SAVING LUCIA

# SAVING LUCIA

by

Anna Vaught

**Bluemoose**

Copyright © Anna Vaught 2020

First published in 2020 by
Bluemoose Books Ltd
25 Sackville Street
Hebden Bridge
West Yorkshire
HX7 7DJ

www.bluemoosebooks.com

British Library Cataloguing-in-Publication data
A catalogue record for this book is available from the British Library

Paperback 978-1-910422-56-4

Hardback 978-1-910422-55-7

Printed and bound in the UK by Jellyfish Solutions

For the family of nursing sisters of Roscommon
(later Massachusetts), who cared for Lady Violet Gibson
in St Andrew's Hospital, Northampton.

'In every language upon earth,
On every shore, o'er every sea,
I gave my name immortal birth
And kept my spirit with the free.'

*John Clare*, from 'A Vision'

Clare was a patient at St Andrew's General Lunatic Asylum
(as it then was) for twenty-two years, dying there in 1864.

# 1

Violet Albina Gibson, the Honourable, was behind bars, wearing an immaculate black crêpe dress, clasping her finest manners and a lovely lacquered fountain pen, for letters to Churchill and others. She was a criminal because in April 1926, in Rome, she shot Mussolini. And she was insane with it; an assassin with devotions, prayers and visions. Not a steady-handed murderer, but one that broke apart most untidily and could not be trusted. In prison, in Rome, she threw a chamber pot at her guard and a flower press at a crack-brain; for an Honourable lady, such rude things she said. Then there were the screams and intransigence: strange mystical tantrums. And in 1927, when they put her in the mental hospital in England, behind those necessary bars, through which you saw a fine vista—*oh and the borders were lovely this year!*—she would *never* do a jigsaw or embroidery, when instructed for her own good. Only towards the end of her life would she do one thing they suggested: she agreed to stand outside with the birds and encourage them to feed from her hands.

Other than that, a hopeless obdurate virago, a strange dotty old girl, mad with religion. And a danger. Or a nuisance. Or both.

When she was locked up here, at St Andrew's Hospital Northampton—a lovely old house for those I call the *feebles* (I'm one of them, as you shall see)—the case of murder was cleared up altogether. She was pardoned by Benito, once his thugs were convinced she was on her own: just a crazy hag taken leave of her senses, not a killer in a conspiracy. After a beating by Mussolini's baying crowd, prison and the asylum in Rome, and the embarrassment of the Foreign Office and family, this, *this*, what we have now, was the right thing to do. It used to be called the General Lunatic Asylum. Where they put the people like us. There are many lifers here. They give them routine and mahogany; croquet on the lawns and medications to soothe. And bars on the sash windows, which have been denuded of cords, just in case. They must have lost the odd one, surely, but records of lives, as I have discovered, and as I will show you here, can go awry.

But as I was saying: St Andrew's is quite a select place if you have the money, because you get a well-appointed room of your own to be mad in. Featherdown for your tears. Even the illusion of freedom. They are aristocrats, some of the inmates, and all of means. So that's what Violet got. Posh. Still. You are locked in, surrounded by mutes doing crochet. Violet rocked into silence when it was all too much. But sometimes, as you will learn, she emerged and, oh Lord, she was jubilant; full of a reckless imagination. And so it was that in the last days of her last year, when she and I were patients and friends together, she asked me to be her scribe. Violet was determined not to be reduced to hearsay and notes in hospital archives. She was clever, too, and kind. Because she knew, when I arrived, all about me. That I was the dotty daughter of the genius writer. I heard her whisper to me that she felt I had been forgotten; also, that I had reduced myself and if I would only buck up my ideas... And she said: Dear, dear girl! None of that is good enough and I long to set you free!

So this is her story and also mine, in what it gifted to me. Will you come? It will jangle, what with Violet's verbal flights of fancy, but I so wanted to write a more-or-less true story. My own previous work, my pretty, inchoate novel, had all been burned up by the family, I feared, so I tried like I had never done before and became Violet's scribe. Sometimes I took notes from her, direct. Sometimes I listened in to visitors, the medical staff or the most lucid of the other inmates. I patiently assembled and edited and imagined, just as Violet had done with her memories and the tales she needed to tell. I worked like crazy and then I was sane enough.

This is how it began. When the old demented crone tried to find some peace and to save me. When she'd done with trying to change history.

Oh, she was quite a girl!

# 2

St Andrew's Hospital: fine gardens, a curved and concealing road, because we needed to be kept away. Trees aplenty and, in her last days, an old lady feeding the birds. Her *passerines*, she called them. Loved them. Staff turned it all into a treatment, her time with them. Observed, noted and took photographs; communing with the little birds was considered therapy. She was poor with people, so they said.

So this, for the old lady outside, greatcoat to the ears, is therapy. This her place. Inside, a visitor might contemplate barred windows, the shout of antiseptic and of the insane. Jangling keys and that soft slip on linoleum: feet of mad people whose tread and grip are light and uncertain. It looks pretty though, doesn't it, this grand building? St Andrew's Hospital for Mental Diseases was once the General Lunatic Asylum and in later days it will be called a psychiatric hospital. Some extraordinary people have been here—the poet John Clare, poor soul; sometimes he thought he was Byron, sometimes Shakespeare. That does not bother me; all that does is his sadness and the interminable life here, from which he still managed to extract beauty. I call that heroic.

I do know that madhouses are not created the same. The Salpêtrière in Paris housed eight thousand women, most of them forever, and I am sure you'll have heard of the old Bedlam? There's money in it here; we are not bedded in filth. But we are still restrained when we rebel; locked in; obliged to stay here. The old adage that a gilded cage is still a cage must apply. And my heart is broken. I hate the open gates across the lifts, deliberately done like that to give the illusion of freedom—a nasty conceit we see through. I loathe the contrasting bolts on doors and windows, the cacophony of keys and drugs trolley and the rictus smile of one of our nurses here. Did I mention the crochet, the jigsaws? I feel compelled to burn low, because, like Violet, if I expressed my rage and abandonment, it would not work out well for me. Or even if I laughed too loudly! Violet has a mind of what's in her notes. She's described as non-compliant and unable to accept her circumstances. I've been listening in. Well that last bit's funny as all hell, isn't it?

Who would be compliant except the person who gave up?

Who could accept?

So, Violet. Come.

When our failed assassin, the Honourable Violet Gibson, was brought here in the middle of the night, what did she think? Harley Street twice certified her madness. Travelling from Euston and shipping up here in the early hours, did she think it was a new property acquired by her family, all lawns and imposing windows: a country estate? She'd made a long journey from Rome, sister Constance at her side; the meetings with the doctors were desultory: they could see straight away what she was, rumpled old crone. It was *obvious*. But still, she told me, she had thought she was going home once she had submitted to these humiliating ministrations. The prods and glances; cursory utterances that made her want to rage and, back in Rome, she'd been subjected to internal examinations. Why? Did the doctors think she was a hysteric with a wandering womb? Why were such invasions necessary? Surely they could have talked to her and found her in pain, but lucid? Poor thing. She knew life must be different now, but also that Mussolini had let her go and that Winnie and Clemmie and others had buttered him up. She hadn't been planning to kill again but still, she thought, therapeutic care might be tolerable and she would accept medicine and much of it could be married with domestic life in London. Perhaps at sweet sister Constance's house. *Yes*, she thought: *that must be it.*

*Little walks; reading; prayer; a modest pension. I doubt I shall try to kill again.*

Not for long could she think it. They went beyond London and home, any home. From Harley Street to Euston and the last train to Northampton. To where?

That crimson first night, exhausted from travelling across the continent, sedation wearing thin, mocked by a cold world, a new era began for her while in Italy her victim rolled his eyes, jutted his jaw and spoke of feeding people to sharks, while the British government praised him and the ladies feted him—even darling Churchill's darling Clemmie. Oh, Benito. Oh, Violet, horrid, horrid crone. Wizened like a friend of Hecate, though not yet fifty. That's how they spoke of her.

That crimson first night, as they swept up the drive of the hospital: terrible. Can you imagine her, in the back of the car and the new world that was coming to her? She thought she was going home and no-one told her otherwise. But no, not home to Mayfair, nor the house in Merrion Square, Dublin. Lady Gibson was never going to see the outside world again, so it was said. Too much trouble.

Pleasantries would have been exchanged, notes handed over and a valise. In it were Violet's simple crêpe dresses, demure pinafores; a shawl she loved. No Lebel revolver, as had been tucked away inside her nightdress when she arrived in Rome, in early 1926. No, of course. Books were to be sent on, but there were her copies of Vasari's *Lives of the Artists* and Alban Butler's *Lives of the Saints*. She loved to look at the first, and particularly those paintings on which she could meditate, those that suggested a mystical devotion. Like the work of Fra Angelico. The second, she later told me, provided inexpressible comfort.

That night Violet was shown to her room and told to prepare for bed. There would have been a sleeping draught she would have been unable to refuse; the acrid smell of the place assailed her; insanity leaching in and out of the walls with the sighs of desperation coming from those permanently incarcerated, encaged. She fell asleep, not like the drift she might have felt as a younger person, or when she was on retreat with the Jesuits, drenching herself in the faith she was so desperate for. No: this was a cold fall down a cliff face. *Down.* Down some more.

Did she note, before, the bars on the well-appointed sash windows, that the door was locked behind her? Through the night, did she stir and hear the jangling keys of the night staff or screams from others' plangent nightmares? Sometimes, the same old voice; might she have heard it as she fell, that first night in the hospital? The trill of a once-loved woman, stripped down, pared back, her essential self now all loon: I am better now, please take me home! I want to go home.

That was then and this was her, Violet, Lady Gibson, who had tried to kill, the first night of the rest of her life, thirty years ago.

What of now, in the last days of our assassin?

She is dying. I hear her rasping, on the rare days she comes to the day room with all the poor feebles in corners, doing cross stitch and slow jigsaws. Then some days she rallies and is allowed out, watched but unguarded, waiting to feed the birds. She has asked me to be with her there sometimes.

Dr Griffith, who is in charge of this place, has been speaking to Nurse Archer, who is from County Roscommon; she nurses here with her two sisters. Yes, I was eavesdropping. He'd been telling her how one of their patients has a lingering effect on him; he cannot entirely put it into words, this sensible man of letters. Yesterday this patient, whom we have already met, had stood in the hospital gardens. Violet Albina Gibson, the Honourable, daughter of The First Baron Ashbourne (or Lord Ashbourne for ease, respected lawyer and politician, Lord Chancellor of Ireland), late of Dublin and Mayfair before her travels on the continent, almost changing the course of history when she shot Mussolini. She had been out there communing with nature before, it being considered part of therapeutic care since, as you heard, she did not get on so well with people and was sometimes mute.

In recent years, notes confirmed that she had first refused then been off-hand with her relatives, such as her devoted sister, Constance, to whom this was understandably a source of great pain. There had been, they thought, ideas of escape, as she could not be trusted, opined she was being persecuted, as she was detained in a mental hospital (which hardly made sense), and dear Constance had written of the cloud that had fallen on her sister. Now, Dr Griffith is giving account: their patient had chastised staff again and again about how she was being denied the comfort of the Catholic liturgy which she so craved; she had been angry when Dr Makepeace of Harley Street, giving the required second opinion, described her delusions as so acute that she should *not* seek to live in the community of nursing nuns at Bexhill to which she had repeatedly asked to go. Disgusted, Violet had spent more and more time outside and then set up camp in a little corner of the hospital grounds.

So this, her therapy, in past years. The only one she ever accepted, far as I can tell.

Standing there, waiting for the birds. Sometimes her carers had wondered, as she stood, if she was right and sane to seek release from the hospital, but second opinion, as I told you, confirmed not. Staff had suggested she might be photographed with the birds, still and calm, sparrow and chaffinch coming to her. Violet spoke little to her carers, but she had asked the nurses, a kind group of sisters from County Roscommon, if they would help her sew little pouches onto the shoulders and upper arms of her worsted coat (for winter) and her blouse and cardigan (for warmer days). To alter her black crêpe dress so that she could feed them; a restful company for her. The pouches were to be filled with crumbs and birdseed; she'd reasoned that the birds would learn to alight on her arms and shoulders. She was right. If you'd looked closely, you might have seen the velvet wing of a passerine sweep across

8

her cheek as it came to rest and feed. Then, Violet smiled. She knew a precious thing: that happiness was simple and caught within a minute like this, and that was all. And she was photographed, for records, in these poses: in no picture would she ever face the camera.

Those pictures are extant, you know. You could see. They will be there in the *Gibson* filing cabinet, near to *Joyce*. I think, you know, that if you're reading this in years to come, long after I'm gone, we'll still be side by side there. Probably in the archives; we'll have moved from the office. But mine had better bloody well not be sealed off, because I'd want you all to know the whole story, the things they put in my notes, letters from the Joyces. And I wonder, too, if we might be buried near each other. I doubt they'll cart me back to Zurich. Or Paris or Trieste. And I'd better bloody well have flowers.

I'm digressing, repeating, so excited am I to be setting this down.

So, Violet in the hospital grounds: look at her, there. Just *look* how the birds of the air love her. Snug on her hands and in the crook of an arm. There were photographs taken where the little creatures blanket her. I love to see those images now. I keep them by me always.

In one particular photograph, though, *Lady Gibson* as the nurses called her, stands, one hand down and across the body, steady of pose, other arm up, raised straight and aimed, as if in prayer, an impulse of religious ecstasy, or in the position to handle a Lebel revolver. But sometimes she was also encouraged to lie back on a deckchair, perhaps as if she were on holiday at Boulogne-Sur-Mer, with her siblings, Mother reading and kind sand; Father, Lord Ashbourne, stage left, writing a speech but present as he could be. Then, she would whisper to him in French, just to him, the story of *The Nightingale* which she knew by heart. Her French so much better than that of her many siblings; her love for her often-absent father possessive and glorious and a source of deep sadness. A nightingale is a

9

passerine, too, you know. When I heard it, in my wandering homes or in hospitals, its melancholy stilled my heart.

Now.

Somewhere else in this hospital, a girl danced, when she first arrived, for rage and a glum beyond words. She was a lusty young thing, adoring her father. But that, also, was then. Now, she is compelled to sit still. Daddy was James Joyce (Violet has read his books and says he's awfully wordy! Oh, look at him, on and on, showing off, she says) and she, in the words of *Finnegans Wake*, was his Lucy Light; cloud girl that rained on the earth; Nuvoletta, a lass. Lucia, named for Lucy, Martyr of Syracuse, patron saint of eyes, light, lucidity: instructing Virgil to lead Dante through hell and purgatory in *The Inferno*. Oh, good things, stopped up! Daddy called her *saucebox* and his *lottiest daughterpearl*. But look what happened to her! She is so sad; unmerried—and he trills her his *Poor Isa*. (I'm fudging from *Finnegans Wake*.) Or rather, this is what I remember because, like all other vestiges of that former life, he's gone to dust. But my imagination has not; it remains, though not, as yet, leaping into the outside world. I'm working on it, to strengthen my mind.

His words help. Daddy's words.

I find I blend in words and phrases from *Finnegans Wake* and, when I do, I feel momentarily less alone and as if I were talking to him. He read to me from that, what he called his *Work in Progress*, until it came into the world. It seems arrogant to say I was his muse and confidante, but I know the book intimately. Knew it then, feel it now. I see myself and I'm cognisant of the language he used, the references to me, his names for me. I am welling up; can't help it. He was my daddy, he wept for me and he died when I could not get to him, when I was incarcerated. He died. And no-one told me.

Oh yes: that *lottiest daughterpearl*. She was me. Then and now.

Did you guess, oh did you now? I am one Miss Lucia Joyce, unmarried, once engaged, big barney with Mother, name of Nora

Barnacle (hereafter, 'the barnacle'—lower case for disrespect; she was dried up as a nun's tit—and the old crustacean never came to see me at any of my establishments, you know) and brother Giorgio; spat brewing with my nephew, the executor of the Joyce estate, if I ever get out of here. Violet says she's heard that, for whatever reasons (Shame, dear!) my letters have been *immolated* (not burned: she loves the old words and I say she's a fine one to say that my daddy was ever wordy). She says I've been immolated, too. She's mad as hell for that, she tells me. Some fellows are not gentlemanly like us, she tells me.

Violet keeps herself to herself, mostly. She's the Honourable and has never dropped the title. She reads all the time: books, papers, journals, pamphlets. This is not a house of intellect, you know. But with her, as long as she's quiet, they let her off the wretched jigsaws and she reads while the old biddies dribble over a picturesque cardboard scene. Of Gibraltar. Or Barmouth. Place called Rhyl, which looks like death to me. So, she's made her *own* house of intellect, God love her. Oh, my father would have loved her. Sam Beckett would have said she was arresting, perhaps put her in a play.

*This place.* It's a stately home for loonies who can pay, but it's also the ditch in *Waiting for Godot*, she says. And a bloody awful play, too, though he must be an interesting boy, your Sam, so I can kind of see how you could, little Syracusa, God love you.

Violet reads her religious texts, scripture, about painting and prayer. She's devout. I'd like to be, I think. She wants me to be; tells me so. Violet is a good girl and a cunning one, who knows the moods of this place, so, when she's been able, she sneaks to my room or whispers at the walls, the sour old door. I hate it. The door, not her. Oh God and the snotgreen sea, she tells of such things and people: mad women of the past. Talks about them as if she knows them and says she can, through thirty years of rattling through her tale and their tale and reading about them—I told you: she reads everything!—well, she can drum up these women. Voices of mad women, junked up to dance for men at the Salpêtrière in Paris or coin a talking cure under a pseudonym. Charcot, Breuer and Freud. Their subjects, the eight thousand harpies in Paris; the woman with snakes for hair when she was mad; the dog barker; sea-shanty-with-a-bottle-of-rum girl. Hysterics they were called. Blanche Wittmann and Anna O.

Oh dear little Lucy Light, she says, mocking a baby voice, pulling me or someone like me out from *Finnegans Wake* (such cheek! The barnacle might have called her a *bog mutten*). I believe you need to meet these women somehow. And, dear girl, you and I have work to do.

Now, don't you wonder what she means, cuckoo old bird? Ha!

She goes on: Do you have a lovely pen for notes, and reams of paper?

I feel like I am entering into something with her and it is... thrilling. But should I be unnerved? She did, after all, learn to use a revolver. She shot Mussolini. In her prison, in Rome, Lady Gibson would not use a chamber pot while a guard was looking. Oh no no no. So she threw it at him. Injured him gravely. I heard she lunged at a maid, back in Mayfair posh of her younger years—and with a knife too, her Bible left open on the sacrifice of Isaac for days. Mad and bad? Here, she went for old Miss Drool (don't know her real name; the drool put me off an introduction) with a mop. Right on the head. Why did she do such a thing, she was asked. *Because,* (set this down someone) *a gentleman does not strike below the waist.* Blank looks and only confusion from Dr Griffith. One said: Ah, she's mad, mad; doesn't know a dachshund from a doily.

*No,* thought I. *They are wrong.*

*She knows exactly what is happening. Her imagination is diamond brilliant and Holy Mary, that was just a joke. That's why she laughed.*

*Because she made a joke.*

When we are walled up, forced to knit a monotone blanket when we would chart a blowsy, expensive galleon across the Irish Sea and back again before dinner, then look what happens! We will come to this again. And to Miss Lucia Joyce. And others. I feel it and she makes me know it.

I don't think Violet will last much longer, but how glad I am that we have this time. She's been here nearly thirty years; just a few for me, although I can tell you I've done the rounds. And you'll see. I'll walk you through the drugs and confinements. Straitjackets.

For now, picture a small gravelled corner and an old lady thinking hard. She'd stood out there, still hours, for many days, being a good girl.

Violet Gibson, the Honourable, the mad. She's been walled up. It's what you do for those with delusions of grandeur, who have assumed holy insight (which adds up to psychosis), bashing a prison warder over the head with a chamber pot and a dear old crazy with a mop; lunging with a knife, a flower press, whatever weaponry is to hand! She's a frigid; she's a clever; a rustling old bird; capable of absconding, self-harm, homicide and jokes at the wrong juncture.

Can't tell a hawk from a handsaw, probably.

That's what they say.

They're wrong.

# 3

You'll want to know why she did it. Why she shot. You'll need a proper story arc, won't you now? In our talks, this is what I learned.

Violet believed Mussolini was a monster and that others would continue to be fooled by him. Wasn't she right? I might argue that if she'd managed the final shot, in Rome 1926, then the world might never have known what he'd got up to; his crimes, at that point, were not beheld by statesmen. He was yet to be revealed for what he was; Churchill yet to change his mind; the mob yet to run on him. Don't you think that would be self-sacrifice of the highest order on her part? She'd kill him and the horrors he had made might not be known, while she'd just be a locked-up mental case.

Violet thought that there was a place for a lawful, just killing and that she would, in her Christian faith, martyr herself. She recounted this to me: Psalms 55: 23. *But thou, O God, shalt bring them down into the pit of destruction: bloody and deceitful men shall not live out half their days; but I shall trust in thee.* And I, my dear, shall help.

And the evidence was there, if only they had looked. Violet had written in her notebook during her time in the Regina Coeli prison, Rome, awaiting trial, that she had been following God's orders; that she was compelled to do what she did. Taunted by another inmate in the prison—*Viva Mussolini ha ha ha!*—scraps of paper pushed under her door or waved under her nose—Violet attacked, pushed beyond bounds, giving her victim, one Ida Ciccolini, a trip to the infirmary with concussion following a lunge with the flower pressing equipment they'd been using.

No, she told me: It was against the will of God that Mussolini should continue to exist!

The lunge with the flower press at poor old Ida (Not so! said Violet: She was what they call in Italy a *cagne intrigante;* a scheming bitch who nonetheless played nicely for the guards, while my crime took on the gloss of madness!) did not serve her well. Meanwhile, she told me, Austen Chamberlain continued to praise the monster.

Violet said: Can you imagine, my Lucy Light? Oh, he was the saviour of Italy. I heard that when Lady Chamberlain accompanied her husband to sojourns with the monster she wore her fascist brooch on her summer-weight cloche hat, or on the fox fur collar she added in winter. And news greeted me that Ronald Graham, our ambassador, merrily called me a lunatic in his special audiences with Mussolini; saying, moreover, that *himself* was too great, too fine a man to countenance violence or ill treatment of me. Ha! Did they not know of clubs and ditches and the brutal fascist boot in the face? *Who was mad here*? But I must say I was not entirely innocent: I hammed it up, now and then, the insanity. It was a form of righteous power. I'd been too long a prisoner!

It was disturbing to hear—of course, of course—but I understood rage and also that Violet had purpose with some logic and grace, if only they had listened.

Her world, also, was grown dark. Father dead after a slip in the park, a bang on the head: such a dull way to go for an eminent man. Mother too; Violet's fiancé, unnamed, hidden and gone: the nurses themselves whispered about this. I heard them, for she was a favourite of theirs. They said her illness and the shots were connected to disappointments in love: the most painful kinds of lovers' tiffs. These things had made her reckless, they thought; she was animated by pain as well as zeal. In the first part of 1926, she had an aim in sight but if it killed her, then so be it. Nurse Archer, from County Roscommon. And her two sisters. Yes, Violet was a great favourite of theirs. I heard that too.

All of this, what I thought, the whispers of the nurses, and Violet's own accounts, we spoke of.

Yes, said Violet when we talked it out: A fair summation. Also, somebody had to kill Mussolini and I got closer than anyone else, don't you think?

As she has commented, who was certifiable here? Why did they consider her mad, and not him? Oh, poor lonely Lady Gibson.

So, I had begun to tell you about the birds. There was a little place in the grounds at St Andrew's which she had made her own. Looking outward, she'd be jostling her fingers gently to make the little birds come. Her passerines recognised her immediately and alighted. She would go there, twice a day, little pouches on her clothes filled with crumbs and some bird seed Dr Griffith procured for her. He'd said *procured* as if it were Beluga or opium, off the medical record. These fellows! Do they think they are indispensable?

At night, she told me, she reached and reached until she saw the swallows of summer and in the swallow, she told me, there is such magic. I didn't understand that, at first.

The little corner that Violet monopolised was just in front of the main hospital building, on the gravelled drive but in sight of verdant tree, grass and bush, and Violet would stand there, stock still, for a long time. Of course, they had had to observe her, but in this time she remained trouble free, though mute, or sometimes mumbling (or so it seemed to an inattentive observer) and distant, seemingly locked into her faraway land. Or perhaps still, in her sorry state, contemplating how she was part of history: the woman who failed to kill herself, for sure, but also Mussolini. Locked away, unjustly, so she thought, poor old crone.

I would listen to her mutterings, and scribe best I could, and they were fascinating. And the point was, they weren't the mutterings of a crack-brain. She was telling a story and coming to terms, in her last days. And I do think, looking back, that being outside freed her, though she was never not captive.

Thus it went, from Violet:

A woman! Fancy, a woman! were Il Duce's words on understanding who shot him. The Fascist magazine *L'Assalto*—a dirty rag; I would not dignify its name with anything else!— mocked such creatures: women of the third sex. Old repulsive women... How dare they? They do not know what we suffer and how we are scorned!

That rag, raged Violet, muttering privately to herself (well, I was there, I was there! She'd invited me as witness). Its own filthy words I wanted to wipe off the face of the earth in one skirmish. Ah! *Women like me*! Horrid; a pollution; damaging menfolk, the beauty of Italian skies, our fathers: ugly women, like suffragettes or Sinn-Feiners; dirty nihilists who might come from Russia or Ireland. Who would want women such as these? What could these women know?

I knew men—Lucia, dear girl, are you listening and scribing? You did too: I know it!—the touch on my skin and a camellia at dusk; once, jasmine and something lingering, something so fine. I have known eyes and sighs and tears and love in darkened rooms on damask. It was my fiancé and I can never tell. Mother never knew, nor my sister Constance, brothers Willie and poor, poor Victor. An artist: not like Fra Angelico, no: bold and modern like the man who painted us: Violet—I; me: us—sisters—on the boat on a lake in Compiègne, Willie's house in France: Roy de Maistre: that was him. My brother Willie's painter guest, bold-splashed like Gauguin in Tahiti. And as for my own poor dead artist boy: I cannot say his name, but at night I consider his bold lines of charcoal at dawn; the things he could do. Oils on canvas, but where are they now? And maybe his colours were one with the saints: green, gold, pomegranate, that salmon pink which is flushed love and devotion. Oh, I have known love.

*Decent* love. As delicate as the linnet's wings at dusk.

Mussolini said to Clara Petacci—and I hate him still, bold monster—he said, *Oh Clara, your kisses stun me and kill me!* in dull amatory cant. Ugh! And she writing to him as a fourteen-year-old girl, back then, Lungo Tevere Cenci, Rome, 1926, just after I shot him and when I was making history: *Oh Duce, I offer my life to you! My beautiful, glistening Duce!* She said I was a wicked soul, my crone hands trying to take a beautiful destiny from a glittering Italy. But oh: glittering, indeed. Strung up with him, dead meat, on the scaffolding at the Esso station and nothing glittered, nothing was beautiful then. Dirty, not decent.

And Violet raged on. I mean, she's hard work to listen to, but she's captivating, don't you think? Sam Beckett might have been proud of what she said next: Mad. Wholly? Mad but north north-west. Am I? Knowing the difference between a hawk and a handsaw. Or not knowing it at all? Or not mad at all?

It was here that the old girl took a breath.

But no-one hears Violet, do they? Her soul rumbles on.

Mussolini was untroubled by such. I think, and Violet agrees, that he was all appetite and want. A hawk looking, always, for his dinner.

*Sotto voce*, Violet. But you know, at least, that *I* was noting.

She is a consumer of books, magazines, whispered stories and conversation; always has been, will be to her dying day. Perennially far more aware than her captors of current affairs. Do they know this, those who care for her?

Her sister, Constance, came last year and it was a good visit, Constance told the staff. She brought with her a story book from childhood, with Violet's name in it, which Mother used to read to her daughter, to all her daughters, at their house on Merrion Square in Dublin, sometimes on their carriage rides along the lanes of Dalkey, where Violet remembered a patch of damp moss, a dropping briar, and that once a dormouse peeped from a hole in the lovely high walls; sometimes at the summer estate her father, Lord Ashbourne, had taken at Boulogne-Sur-Mer. Violet loved it, the story book, and dear Constance remembered. *Fairy stories of Hans Christian Andersen* and, in particular, The Nightingale, oh, sweet, serene, enchanted passerine.

Violet is thinking about The Nightingale now. She remembers it, word for word, and now mouths its ending as the emperor promises to break the artificial bird into a thousand pieces and cries to the real bird: You shall sing whenever you like!

I know it too, from Daddy when he read; from the barnacle, too. I read it to Giorgio when we were little, in a different country—and I don't just mean the past or, you know, beyond our prison. Let me continue. Here's Violet, again, as I note her, telling the story of this sweet bird, consoling the emperor: I will sing to cheer you and to make you thoughtful too; I will sing to you of the happy ones, and of those that suffer too. I will sing about the good and the evil, which are kept hidden from you. One thing I ask you. Tell no-one that you have a little bird who tells you everything; it will be better so.

Then the nightingale flew away.

And:

Good morning little birds, says Violet now.

Still and for a long time, hands outstretched against the rime and the cold breeze; an azure morning: the birds come to her. So still.

He, Dr Griffith, remarks (I am still listening in!) that days ago, when she came in from the cold, she said this. She said, *The passerines, Dr Griffith, just so*, hollow-eyed but clear, like a sage, like she is. And he had thought, I bet, *That is a beautiful word.* I saw the look in his eyes. Then he said (they think I've gone to dust, but oh no, I get about and listen in) Nurse Archer, you were aware of her letters to her sister in law, Marianne? Lady Gibson wished her to contact the Home Secretary and petition for release.

And?

Well, and nothing. Marianne had not forgiven her for past wrong—and of course she's a source of shame and embarrassment to the family—so her letters were forwarded to Constance and now they are in the filing cabinet here, should you wish to look more. The Home Secretary was never told. Lady Gibson was clever and included the photographs we took of her with the birds; to prove her sanity and that she is peaceful, I should think. I doubt she realises, though, that she has been thwarted. That none of her campaign or request letters got out. I think she has given up trying to escape and of course she's been ill for some time. I thought she was going at several points, so it is as if she has a last lease on life here. She insisted on going outside to feed them again and we let her, though she is still very frail.

That was kind of you, Doctor. Poor old thing.

But Dr Griffith, though convinced of the need, always, for Violet to be detained here, though sure of his work and of her delusions, is purpled under his eyes because the case of this murderous aristocrat troubles him. Of that I am sure. And now he says to Nurse Archer, She reminds me of someone. She is exalted; her pose is like that of Giotto's St Francis. Do you know this work? And I think she speaks to those little creatures, tells them stories. She is feeding the birds with her words; English countryside become the Predella at Pisa. Poor withered old thing.

And Nurse Archer says to him, Yes, I do know the work, Doctor. Ah, but Napoleon looted that, the Predella, didn't he? My dear man, (they have been friends and confidantes a long time, so such is their relative informality) it has been in the Louvre since 1813. Not in its home—displaced, like poor old Lady Gibson.

*She's showing off to him*, I think. Maybe I should try that, too. I reckon I know what to do with a man. I've danced Salome, you know.

So then, Dr Griffith, who sometimes paints, he says: She keeps *The Lives of the Artists* by the bed. Her sister Constance, I think, brought her little cards—Fra Angelico—and when I saw her the other night, she asked me to lean in: Look, Dr Griffith: the lapis lazuli; the vermilion. He said, you know, Fra Angelico, he said that he who does Christ's work must stay with Christ always. And she whispered that Fra Angelico was bathed in tears whenever he went to paint a crucifix and she took up hers—you have seen it, by the bed?—and cried and called for Mary. I had... had to steady my nerves. She called me back and these were her words:

Dr Griffith. I know I am going to die and I know you think that I am mad and always have been. Please, say no more. But look at this. You see my cards? Fra Angelico *The Annunciation*. I have more than one because he painted this scene time and again. The dove is there, of course, cascading through the golden light from angel to virgin, but what else do you see? Look at both. There in one, not in the other?

I said that I detected differences in form, in foliage, in colour. I wasn't sure what she was getting at, so I observed that, of course, there were bound to be differences.

Look up, she said, look central. Do you see the little swallow, there? I am not sure it even looks at Mary as she receives the wonderful news, but it is sharp and clear and ready to fly. And it belongs to that most poetic group: the passerines. And sometimes Fra Angelico paints it and sometimes it is not there at all. I like to think of where it went. To hotter places to tell of the news? To commune with others, to rest with the other birds even, here, as I stand outside in my little spot and feed them, arms outstretched, as I like to do. To help me?

Of course it is all hysterical enough: neurosis, confusing times; noticing insignificant detail that a fifteenth-century friar surely cannot have meant to be... to be so portentous? But again, there is something about her. No, not just the belief and the mumbling of altarpieces. It's something to do with those birds. I cannot get it out of my head.

And Dr Griffith (I've studied him well) is also a reader of many esoteric and abstruse texts, though he does not notice or believe the detail he should, and he says, though sensible Nurse Archer rolls her eyes, and it might be a surprise to the reader to hear of this from Dr Griffith, that history shows you never can tell from where or from whom imagination may body forth or epiphany may spring, The creation myth of birds; the primordial sea—the *Psalms* tell of it, the mire, it is told of constantly in the Old Testament. Sometimes Jesus, sometimes a bird descends into the sea and brings up a portion of the silt and so land is created. If... He pauses because he is uncomfortable and under scrutiny: It is as if there is something she knows which we don't. I hear her whispering to the birds here and they come to her as, I think, they would not to me. It's as if she is creating something out there. Land? A stable place that she has created. And—please forgive me, Nurse Archer: this is hardly the kind of thing to put on notes—I wonder, in her strange way, does she still mock the man she shot, blown through with the passion of Christ? He was a strange one. He pardoned her, you know that? Il Duce had foreseen his death, but hoped for a beautiful woman as his assassin, not an old crone. I read about it.

He adds: And I do think, if she had a fair shot at him, were he alive now, she'd do it again.

Are you tired, Dr Griffith? asks the nurse.

I think that I am. But listen. He forgot her; everyone has forgotten her, I meditate upon that. But she was there at extraordinary times and lived through such things and he, Mussolini, was a monster. What if she had not missed? The lives she would have saved. She must know of what came next. It's odd: we, her carers, say she is not a companion of reality, and yet Lady Gibson is up to the minute on current affairs, primed and analytical. We have magazines, papers here; have always had. Lady Gibson insists on it all, too. And news from the outside world is exchanged, so... She has a sort of confidence. I might be her doctor, but had I been his, Mussolini's, who would I have said was more mad?

I like Dr Griffith. I don't know if it's a recent development or even the effect of Violet, but he's tentative. I mean, he's locked us up and medicated us; forced us to try croquet at the summer jamboree and tried to get me to play the cornet for the asylum band when I was too stiff to offer a little dance or run the dash for old women at the same event—such execrable things—but he does try. And his uncertainty is appealing. I'm less keen on this nurse, which is not one for the sisterhood. She steers him away from uncomfortable talk, which is why she says, Oh now there's a question! Who was more mad? I'm not sure you should trouble yourself with such thoughts.

But they're pertinent, aren't they? he says. To our work here? Yes, but I am tired. Now, Lady Gibson. She says she likes to talk to Lucia, Miss Joyce, you know. She has only been here two years. Poor girl with a dancer's poise; still talking, sometimes, of Him.

And that is?

Beckett, Samuel, you know, the writer, of sorts. Not really to my taste. That godawful play about waiting, three years back. But I gather he's important now and he has visited a little. He was a friend, an acolyte of her father's and apparently Beckett and Lucia may have been lovers.

(I hate listening in when they're talking about me, coining and writing me.)

Her father. And that was?

You must know! James Joyce.

Ah yes. But he has never been, has he? I assumed him dead. And her mother? I do remember her brother here, Giorgio, sad eyed, not so friendly, but deliberate. He came once and it was not so pleasant. I did not see him again. He complained that we were asking his sister to be involved in menial tasks. I did explain that this was right and proper; helped patients to partake properly in this community and he said no more, though he was frosty.

This was abysmal to hear, but they're right enough.

They forget, goes on Dr Griffith, those who are on the outside. Who are at liberty. I am told that her father would have moved heaven and earth for her, but when he died suddenly, well... Come with me. Things to do and she, Violet, pulls at my heartstrings. Birds. The songbirds. Speaking of freedom in the garden and finding freedom for Lucia. Yesterday, when I talked to Violet, to Lady Gibson, she told me that Lucia should dance, in an espalier pose in the garden, surrounded by the sweet birds, like a thriving fruit tree, in bloom, and with its limbs outstretched. She doesn't know the real world now. Do *either* of these poor birds? At least that is what I think sometimes. And yet... as Lady Gibson's fond of telling us, she has lived in important times: the things she has not seen but, ensnared, mad, here, *the things she has*. And it gives me pause; troubles me, even. The stories I don't know and the glint in her eyes of the stories she does. But enough. Would you go to her, Nurse Archer; see that she's steady? She's such an elegant lady, isn't she? But I think that this is her last gasp now: she is near the end.

Oh, and don't forget, nurse. Do not call her Violet. Keep the title, please. She is very particular about that. And it's fine for Lucia to be with her. I've seen her scuttling about with pen and notebook. I don't know what they're up to, but I doubt it could do any harm.

And so the nurse goes and comes. I've had it up to here with all the Joyce family analysis and their pity about Beckett, I must say. You know, I'm poor this and poor that. Daddy's dead, Mother never visited me anywhere, Giorgio was frosty, Sam jilted me for his Frenchwoman and only had me because he was Daddy's acolyte. And on and on. I'll jabber it before you do!

And then the nurse, Nurse Archer, to Violet, she says this:

Lady Gibson? Are you feeling fine? Do stay outside. It's set fair so you could walk in the garden. You may keep Lucia with you.

And Violet begins to whisper; the nurse hears it only as rustling and is not sure even if it is there. Thus, like a poem:

What balm and blessing. It is morning dear. Do stay outside!

I cannot go beyond, you know, but oh, others cannot go beyond their rooms.

Pardon, Violet? Could you speak a little louder to me?

I am nearby, and listening, scribbling with a wild energy.

Nurse, thank you, but I have to whisper in these circumstances. And please retain my title. Decorum is essential in a lunatic asylum.

The admonished nurse retreats inside, to watch her from the window.

Violet whispers—the nurse's arrival made the birds skitter and scatter, but now they return and, as they do, hand across her body and hand raised to the sky, Violet begins to talk again, and this is what she says: it comes out in a torrent, because she's had an extended period of saying nothing. It comes out in broken lines, sometimes like sprung rhythm, sometimes like she's mocking Joyce, Daddy, sometimes, well we just have to huddle up, keep up. Oh, I could see she was rattled today, upset and crying. I didn't take down everything she said, because you'll wander off, reader. All a bit like Lucky. You know, in Sam Beckett's play. *Qua, qua, qua*, like the poor gibbering fellow says. But here's a flavour as Violet speaks, as she narrates. No, as she *curates* her story:

So early, bundled against the pretty hoar, the rime, I will feed the birds. It will be comfort, if cold, against a bare tree and a pale lavender sky that did not know me. My greatcoat tugged up against my ears, with its hospital smell and them there watching to see, I suppose, that I have been good; that I've treated the little creatures with care and fed them from the crumbs I secreted, every day, in my pockets, forbidden I expect, I am sure, but known about and accepted, glossed over. I like that man, Dr Griffith. I hear him talk about his paintings and about the poetry he reads; about gnostics, creation myths, demi-urges, Cathar heresies, so much, so deep. I think, sometimes, he sees me and he suspects.

Oh the things I have seen! Nancy Astor cartwheeling at Cliveden! King George taking tea with my father. Theosophists and Madame Blavatsky's cronies; Mary Baker Eddy, she who cracked off the New Scientists, hitting her head on a New Hampshire pavement and being sure, after that, that everything, her own illness, wellness, was only of the imagination and those New Scientists babbling because they'd found a religion! My mother loved her, Mrs Eddy, though Mark Twain said it was all Eddy-gush and oh that, in the end, was right. Oh my dear girl. The things!

I felt the warmth of Mary smile on me and a little white woman in the corner of the room when THEY weren't looking. Oh, for Mass and the liturgy I crave! But, as I was saying, no, nothing is glossed; no shine and no footnote, endnote, coda. I mean, they pretend, rough handed, not to notice. But then, of course, of course, you will have known what I meant. I am so old and my strength and intent are hardly a sightly thing.

The staff here watch me, *me* as I tell you, Lucia, and if they do not know the fire in my heart, they see a glow about my eye and opine confidently that it is madness, derangement's augur and the incipient psychosis; throwing an implement or breaking a bird. I expect they saw my arm raised, in the photographs they took of me with the birds, and thought I was remembering the gun and that monster, that day, at the Palazzo dei Conservatori, his chest puffed out, chin up. And people burst into song!

The poets and the artisans,
The landlords and the peasants,
With pride at being Italian

Swear faith to Mussolini!

They were young and fresh; just students, bonny and full of life.

He saluted and I fired.

But no: that is not what I am thinking about now; they are wrong. They don't know the power of what's out there. My hand stretches out to the passerines—how fine that word is—and it is prayer; supplication and oh! The world of the imagination. No. *They don't know the power of what's out there.* Or even the joy compressed about my heart, as one little creature finds the crumbs in my hand.

Nurse Archer comes to check and brings with her a trainee, another of these Irish nurses; I hear tell two—or three?—of them are sisters; they're from Roscommon. Nurse Archer says: These are Lady Gibson and Miss Lucia Joyce, you know, who...

Will she snap the little bird's neck? asks the other. It must be a risk?

*Fool.* That's what Violet's thinking, by the look she gives, as they retreat inside. And she continues in her reverie, this strange monologue:

I know these little creatures and they warm me. In this contracted world, they are the only thing, and my crumbs, so hidden and only mine, only now, that have sense and which speak. Songbirds. Passerines. Everything else gibbers and does not make sense in this hot old place. Me, I like the cold; when it bites and then the birds come to feed at my hand, I do good and I am vital, rosy cheeked, in my mind's eye, a girl, she, me, they do not know. They have been heavy on the chlorpromazine, so you see sometimes there are muddles, but I don't know if they are *my* muddles, or those of these new-fangled drugs. Still, it beats those horrid powders I used to be made to snuff up, And of course, it beats being restrained. I must think. *Think hard;* I must make thought crystalline.

So. Lucia, can you hear me?

And yes, of course, I hear the lot, wonderful crazy. And I know the most wonderful story is going to unravel. And I will have the company I crave, we both crave.

Bertha, where are you?

Blanche? Is it *your* turn to put on a show?

Oh, these girls, Bertha, Blanche, are eminent patients. I've been reading all about them. The conversations we have had! You will meet them, too, when we go, when we fly.

Lucia, are you getting this down?

And I reassure her: *of course, of course.*

On she goes in this abstracted poetry of hers:

I am coming and I will send a bird to dive down deep and gather up silt and build us land.

Can you hear me? Oh, I promise.

I have been here such a long time that sometimes I can no longer tell where this place ends and where I begin; I look for the seams, the joins, but I cannot see them; read the books I have; the torn Bible; newspapers I insist upon, and then there are the old letters from my father: *Oh, I am gravely disappointed, but in time you will be healed and recover from the shame of this and from your difficult self, so they tell me.* He ached, like others of his time, from the awful Catholic perversion I had followed in going over to Rome. Now, I finger the handkerchief that once belonged to my mother, round and round: a peony, a hedgerow, an arched trellis where the floribunda thrive. I think of these words and cry. Here: *Mother. Love. Once. Home.* Home it was. A splendid home; a splendid garden with a peony whose scent I adored. Now home is here except, as I said, sometimes I cannot tell where this place ends and where I begin and what continent separates she from I. Or us; me,

Ah, but I know the passerines and they know me.

I think. I think I can feel a plan forming.

When they saw me, that day, the crowd in Rome, I could not stretch out my hands to them, for I held the gun. I was tiny, frail-looking, shabby straggling black crêpe dress, grey old hair and spectacles, not just so. If they, the exultant crowd, saw me, they wouldn't have read in me, my father, great man, the peer, First Lord Ashbourne; they'd not have glimpsed the dirty debutante or the girl on a mission. In my pocket the small revolver was warm and by God, it was willing. They thought I was saluting him—Dear old Muss, saw himself as grand as *Mare Nostrum*. But no! I took aim, pulled the trigger, eight inches away. The deity was astonished, cold eyes meeting mine, blood through the fingers and he staggered. I pulled again and the baying arm-raised crowd all froze. The pistol took a cartwheel in the air and my hair was pulled and I was trampled as the acolytes came for me. Was it the shot, or when I lay down, not even deflecting the blows, that cried *she is mad, mad, mad*?

My grimy spectacles, inches away, cracked like the toffee shards of my childhood, the broken silver bicycle in the road and little Violet crying, but I closed my eyes and I did not resist while they killed me. Then I was alive, I, me, her, whoever, while Rome in Tiber melted and I was in that cell on the muddy banks and my interrogation began.

Violet is crying; shaking a little: struggling to compose.

Jesus, Mary and Joseph! And they thought *I* was insane! *He* thought he was Christ! Pope Pius XI said Benito was a man sent by providence! God would call this madness! Mussolini? I asked the men: Are you sure it was me?

I thought I could hear him laughing as he mopped his grazed nose and oiled that brazen physique to strut and curse and rule and be Christ ready for a languorous crucifixion. Mad man!

Here is what notes might say if I were Doctor Gibson in charge of the loony bin: *General paresis; malarial therapy indicated. If resistant, treat with more modern deep sleep therapy, barbiturates to be discussed with pharmacy* or something like that. Instead, he was Caesar, until he got crucified, upside down on the carcass of a petrol station.

So, I pace. And I am here. Old trees; frost. A long way down from that Roman spring. Being here, where I pace is, of course, what you would expect mad people to do and where you would expect them to be. I look at the walls and the glass in the windows and the bars across them, hint of rust; tang of acid and a tiny corrosion where a little spider might make its den. Outside, even on the days when I am told I cannot go outside, I watch the lime trees, pollarded like we are by a church and I am cascading in my tiers of dress down the path and my father looks at me, bride on his arm, and knows that I am the finest he has seen, his beautiful girl, and then He, my lost lover, the artist, is waiting for me and we are inside the church and it is well and He lifts my veil and the congregation says *Ahhh*, and no, he is gone and so too my father all to grey mist and we are waiting, waiting for all time, aren't we? I mean Godot, of course! We are in a play in which nothing happens, twice. Or more, in fact.

Violet, enough of those digs at me. At Sam.

I am sorry; I should not make that frayed old joke. Not-joke. I make it to you, Lucia, here, through the walls, about the Irishman and about the waiting she will do, as happens in that godawful play of his—though I do see in it a helpful metaphor for this place. Her father is gone, but Nora, Mother, will come; Oh yes, she says, she will come, she will come, though I don't know how, and it will be changed and He, Sam Beckett, will come and I will leave here and speak French and eat olives and good bread and sausage and drink wine and my sleep will be natural, there in the streets and in the long grass. Me, dancing. Oh yes. Then I'm so strong. And there will be trains to glide away and Giorgio will come and Mother—but of course, oh yes, yes, she is dead—and the ghost of Father to thank me again and again for *The Wake*—Lucy Light, Muse, I, always! The Irishman will leave his Frenchwoman and He will love only me and see that He was wrong; it wasn't just my father, genius and the sun to orbit. Ah no, I think Lucia would say in that thick voice of hers. Not like one of us, one of ours is it? Voice dipping and sweeping low, gutturals like furrows, but still the cast in her eye spellbinding. Did you know that

St Lucy, for whom she was named, is the patron saint of the blind?

I was taking notes, all right, but I said to her, I shouted at her: Shut up, shut up. You are laughing at me, my Lady, and I will cry and scream, because who would not. I hate you now. Doing my voice, hearing you pretend to be me, recite the things I said or want to say!

But she's right. She shouts now: You've got to get this out, dear girl, if you're to have a chance at freedom—and oh yes, she's right.

Violet continues. God, I am coming to love her now. She says: Lucia, I have seen many things. Once, in the crepuscular hour, I swear I saw you, Lucia/Lucy with wings, gliding like an angel. I think I have that right. *Lux.* Light. But *you*, as I, have been in darkness. And anyway, we're lunatics: you're a walled-up martyr to your family and it's wrong, wrong, wrong. Drenched in phenothiazines, the new things. Sedated, hypnotised, trying to scream at the bars and the faked-freedom open doors on the lifts, but unable to because they stopped it up, that proper wail. I heard on the grapevine that people are starting to witter about you, even write about you. Say that you've had the celebrity treatment because you hobnobbed with Jung and some say you're schizophrenic and others that you're just hopelessly sad, locked in: lost.

I say: I am coming to love you and writing this down, but shut up shut up shut up because its pain is almost intolerable.

Violet is in tears as she thinks about her father and the outside world and the loves that died. She cries: And I am not a bride and so my father is not there and really I was telling only about what I can see here, through the ochre bars, and they are lime trees and I know that, under their leaves, life clings tenaciously in the ladybird larvae in their shade and so the leaves are sticky and the little life is hidden there, baby bigger than its mother, its father, then smaller again and pretty, so tiny, but diminished in size as it grows in strength and stature, as I am myself diminished, and never was a big thing to them, or Father or Mother, the man I shot. I will die here. I know it now. It is my forever. But Lucia, do you want it to be your forever, too?

Oh dear girl; dear sweet girl. I am rambling. Apologies to all. Am I worthy of staying *the Honourable*?

I do wonder, Violet. And the thought of St Andrew's being my forever, now what choice do I have? That is what I say. I, Lucia.

She smiles at me, wry old bird and laughs: And yet. And yet. I see possibilities, even now.

You know, Lucia, that I can hear you muttering sometimes? You say, *Introibo ad altare Dei. Ad Deum qui lætificat juventutem meam* and I think, *Psalms*. Then I think, *is she just finishing the line in Ulysses or is she going somewhere, hands outstretched to our God*? You cry for your daddy, say that he is the light, that you are his wonder child. Momentarily, he warms any memory of your destitution; I hate to hear it, that sorrow. And I wonder: would he have allowed this? I've been a bit disappointed in fathers. In families, I must say.

As for me, my coat is desiccated, but warm. I am sure they have disinfected it. Do they think I have lice? Am unclean, to be shovelled off? Boiled up, even?

Oh God, she's off again:

Footfalls.

Sometimes I think I am being buried—under smells that I did not make and were pressed upon me and on my clothes by others.

The sheets are stretched linen, like corpse skin, brushed by imaginary lavender; really-there hard carbolic. But my imagination is deft and clever, for living in this country in our heads is how we survive. I am looking at the building now and I can tell and feel the old moss of walls, clover and summer sweet; a beautiful green summer world to go tumbling in, but so long ago now, in Ireland and my home. Oh: I can feel the soft places behind the sand dunes in France and the pretty foliage in London parks. I can feel the shape of a gentle breeze bringing the wide world in—such bold corn and wheat in the antiseptic corridor, oh and I know, as they cannot, that the pills, so elaborate, of morning and evening are like little buds and buttons in autumn; or pebbles on a summer beach; red pyracantha for the winter birds: the winter song of the robin, for sure, as he rattled once outside my window at home in Ireland.

As we make our way inside, a nurse goes down the corridor. Time for the drugs. She has jangling keys, later. There are some tough tools in this place. *Time for your medicine* she says to one who dribbles and maffles so. It's Miss Drool, who gets on my nerves: cannot abide madfolk. And I put my hand out to Violet and say: I am sorry, Violet. What's happened to us. And what will have happened to those other women you mentioned, women of the not so distant past.

And she says, Oh Lucy Light, I am sorry too and sorry that I reach this pitch and the words come and they come, like a big knife, a cleaver, coming down; Abraham and Isaac: sacrifice your child for me like the page in my Bible, always open on my desk; evidence, that was. Violet is mad they said—the cleaver; the child; the father; the God—and look, this was her idea: Il Duce, glamour and badness, crucify him and come at him deft and young with a cleaver and they said I had no plan and bound me over and took me away and I am here and it is my forever and the whole world is dirty. Rot.

Was Lucia, *were you*, sacrificed, too?

I'm sorry. I must calm down. I am sometimes mute for long periods (Lucia you are too, I know) and so when the words come, it is like a torrent. I think maybe I sound a bit like an echo of Joyce, although I'm a simpleton, not the genius he was, yes? You think? We could have met, you know, at Howth, my fellow countryman and I, all those years blown back. He wasn't an aristocrat of course, however well he might have written.

To this I say, *Enough Lady Gibson.*

Ah, God love you, Lucia, dear, dear girl. Do you know that I heard you muttering the other week; half sibilating, half singing: Will you miss me more and more as the winding weeks wing by? I think (you see, I read, I read), that this is from *Finnegans Wake* but that you've changed it. Why? Are you not allowed to speak it? Has someone forbidden you? Or do you not remember it right? You drag on your Lucky Strikes: I will wear a rose in my hair! Yes, a flower of the mountain and visit the azure houses... with their gentian gardens... I don't think that's how it went. *Ulysses*, this. Drawing to its close. But hard to tell.

*That's enough about me, Lady Gibson. Enough of the Joyce family analysis.*

And what of me, of my story?

Well now, I am history!

In 1932, when I had been here five years, a song came on the radio. I always had my little radio and my books and papers. I always kept abreast of current affairs knowing that if I didn't, I'd as well be dead. And as I was saying, I heard Flanagan and Allen singing *Underneath the Arches.* Oh, how lovely. And there, in the song, was a spoken piece:

Do you remember when we first sang it? says Allen.

Yes, Ches. We used to sit on a seat with the Thames Embankment behind us. You had a newspaper and read the headlines.

And they read. *Gertrude Ederle, eighteen-year-old American. First woman to swim the Channel... Ashes for England after fourteen years... Irish woman, Violet Gibson, shoots Mussolini in the nose.*

Ah, I was history, recorded history as, downstairs, my notes were updated and they wrote *dangerous, suicidal* or *persecution complex*, the last of which arose because I was angry at being detained in a mental hospital with all the shufflers. Ha! I know I am not always the kindest, but you would have to agree that not everyone is immortalised in a song. I turned up the radio, over the rattling of the drug trolley doing its rounds over uneven parquet floors, and got detention.

*Violet Gibson shoots Mussolini in the nose.*

The injured man forgave me, of course, old crone. Worthy only of his pity. Il Duce. 1926. I heard he wanted to be crucified by a pretty girl, a pretty end for a master, a martyr; got off on it, they said, in language I would not use. It was a passion narrative. Edgardo Sulis: that was it. Described the Duce's parents as Mary and Joseph in regard to Christ. And the children in some schools across Italy were forced to learn their parody creed. I heard it as I prayed and thought that Christ wept; Mary, too.

*I believe in the high Duce—maker of the Blackshirts—and in Jesus Christ his only protector—Our Saviour was conceived by a good teacher and an industrious blacksmith* and on and on and *He is seated at the right hand of our sovereign—from there he has to come and judge Bolshevism* and on and on and *I believe in the wise laws... the... the... the resurrection of Italy—the eternal force. Amen.*

All I did was graze his nose and they bound me up, poor shot, and that cell, at the prison in Rome, was damp and endless; the rats screamed and came for my old feet and then they hurt me and I said *But you always knew it was me* and they, though I'm not sure who, spat in my face and kicked me and I was bloodied and wet and asleep, which then was natural. And they bound me again and brought me here, to a third country, my forever home. I am not saying I was all good and sometimes I did tell lies and make bad confession. But I did not blaspheme. I did not dirty the Passion nor the Creed. I did not spit on the Psalms, either.

Nurse Archer calls to us: Lady Gibson, Miss Joyce, it is rest time dears, but there is no *dear* in her voice; it says, really, *baggage and curse*—and I don't like it anyway: too familiar. Rest is what a child does, when it's overwrought—yet just for a moment I know I will try, from my unnatural sleep, to come up shiny and bathed, wash up clean from the pretty water; and there will be love and friends and a new dress and the church walk and father will be there and sure he will look at me for then I am the pretty, pretty thing. I do dream about such. I know Violet does, too.

Lady Gibson, Miss Joyce, I quite clearly told you it was BEDTIME, dears. Do you hear me? Please do as you are asked.

Who does she think she is? Perhaps I'll pull rank, says Violet, then: Lucia, dear dear girl, you are the only one here who would understand me.

Doctor Griffith has allowed us to sit together in a corner of the day room (the parlour they call it; more homely, I gather). It was the quiet time of day before wash and bed when we were supposed to be calm and exchange greetings with the others; to pick up one of the books there or do a jigsaw—but tonight we could just sit. A tear rolled down my cheek because that was all we had to do, friends. Violet told me. About her bed and her past; how she would play with her dolls house and imagine she inhabited it and was safe in Lilliput. How, when she looked at the clean, plain blankets on her hospital bed, she would think of these other things. She said, You know, tonight I was looking at the blankets on my bed and then I saw the counterpane of childhood there. My rocking horse in a corner; the gabled dolls' house with the porcelain blancmanges and plates of ham and salad, shiny and always perfect. And the tiny people, busy and at home in beds and drawers and on the stairs and happy wherever they were which was where I had put them. Can you imagine? Blancmange and legs of ham and salad for breakfast, if you wanted! Did you have such things, girl?

I said, No, my life was so wandering, a dolls' house would have been too big. I remember books, a little bag of stuffed and quilted things; bracelets. That is all.

And on Violet goes, pressing my hand: But I was saying, the counterpane on the high gabled iron bed, with lavender bags from my mother hung at each apex, each nadir. So pretty. On the counterpane of childhood, I could trace loops and countries;

I imagined the grouping hoops like wedding bands, double wedding bands, true love. It was my country of hope, not the tree of you didn't, a flower of you weren't, you sang when you shouldn't, you are, you will be, dirty old rat-bitten crone. La la la. The rings had little bells, such sweet bells and violets, my name, my friends cupping and cradling the bells and so I would lounge in this country and it was big, beyond anything our eyes can see. And then the universe was not malicious; it was at worst benign, maybe laughing and with us, not at us, life, death and other tuppenny aches. The fuss, the bother and trouble. So, I was looking at my bed, tonight, St Andrew's not the garden in Ireland (oh but of course you knew) and seeing a counterpane above the boiled grey blankets, felted with the hard wash and the stretched linen corpse sheets. I hate them beyond expression and into silence.

But I am being bad. I promised to be a good girl.

You know, they could have hanged me, out there, in there; instead this incarceration and boiled wool beds and corpse linen. But Il Duce, grazed by my bullets, he thought he would live forever. I thought of Ozymandias, trunkless legs lost to sand and a wind-blown inscription,

They hung the man up by his heels, the man I shot; he never expected that. They never do, you know!

Lucia, dear girl, dear silly girl, let us talk about you. I have heard whispers from the walls. I am not supposed to know. It's said that you have been rubbed out. Your letters gone; records destroyed, gone to dust. Burnings. Everyone has forgotten, you poor thing. You had no gun. It is not right. I want to give something to you.

I wonder what. Who loves me, really? I think she's come to the same pass.

And then Violet says, Ah, but we will fly: I have a plan. A sort of trip for mad women like us. I want to save you.

*Save you.*

*Saving Lucia.* I like the ring of that.

And that phrase of hers, it awakens something in me; I cry at its tenderness and my words to her come in a jumble: Father said my body would not could not dance. He was a genius, I know, they say, they know. He said I was good, I wanted ballet, but my body was stiff and cold; I couldn't do. So he said; so he told them. I left. Draw, write. *The Wake.* Tried to draw pretty things for his *Pomes Penyeach.* I was good at lettrines, don't you know? The talk between us, it wasn't so much, just knowing: nods and sighs, a sort of argot. But not so much. I murmured and said I wanted something that was mine but he wanted to look after me. Moulding. Mother did not come again—not after the first time. She forgot me after France, after Ivry, after the first time in the straitjacket. There were men, before, there was Him. Sam. You know who I mean, clever lady. He was also a genius. Left, too. He saw the world for what it was: bad tallow and ashes. But did you know him, in Ireland, or was He gone to Paris then?

That was all a jabber but, as Violet said before, *it had to come out.*

Violet says, Girl, speak roundly, speak softly: speak like a lady, please!

And:

It is not fair, what they have done. Lucia Joyce, they made you not exist, out there. If I were not here, it would go on. But I *am* here. I cannot help everyone, but...

Again, I feel like a door has opened. I haven't been able to speak, poisoned by loneliness and out in a gush. And I haven't been able to cry. Violet says it's the same for her, because there is no cry left.

Now it's almost nightfall and tomorrow, there will be a morning. In a lunatic asylum, time shifts and slides; here are elisions and confusions, but you know it's the middle of the day because it's tapioca, and tapioca is a lunch pudding. I swear they've taken the clocks down and of course some of these crazies don't even notice the appearance of the tapioca. As I told you at the beginning, divisions of time cease to have meaning. But to be aware, if you can, feels like a tiny piece of freedom.

Violet whispers: Lucia, I think that you are clever; incandescent, really. It is a torment. Jigsaws, crochet, little walks. We both dodge those things. Yes, I think you are terribly clever and that you have been cast out and made to stop what made you stridently, ragingly alive. We push our collars up, against the cold, and we go Outside. They must be letting us, because this isn't really allowed, mad with mad. You're in full view of the nurse now. Someone is supposed to be with me, at all times, because I am on suicide watch. And of course, I am a killer. A bad shot, but still a killer. So they are watching. Through a squint, or perhaps I have misunderstood the dimensions of this world and I am in a panopticon.

On, Lucia.

They'd not locked the doors yet and we sneak out in the purple twilight.

I extend a hand and the passerines come and the air is lyrical with rushed beauty. Small miracle: a nuthatch. Seemed like that tiny bird whispered to her. Passerines, she and I.

Back in. Before they see.

One day, because this is our forever place, she and I will be under the sod, near each other; there's no way around it. Northamptonshire is not a place I know; I have never seen it. But we have things we both know, in this hard barren place of boiled wool and no-hope where we have been left. You, my darling, are a mountain in that small body, old before young, screaming poetry, talking about Giottos and I wail with *The Wake* and the dancing vocabulary which was once precious.

Violet says, like a prayer, an invocation, Come to us, passerines. Soon enough, we will come with you.

Oh yes. We rush inside, excited.

Where are Violet and Lucia, Nurse Archer? Are they accounted for? It's not exactly scientific, but at my desk just now I thought... I sensed a disturbance

We are listening in, poor sod. They've yet to bolt our doors. We have been so compliant, so ready to engage that there must have been some latitude for us, we think.

Says Nurse Archer: They are in their rooms, Doctor, and night medicines administered. Both seemed agitated; we have given extra, as per notes.

Dr Griffith finds he cannot concentrate, takes up his Bible. Remembers birds of childhood.

Let him see.

Remembers.

As a boy, turn of the century thereabouts, his father made him go to scripture memory competitions. Welsh Baptist family. Now his eyes are moist. *Iesu Mawr*! He was good at scripture. Father made him do it in English, but the boy's Welsh was tidy, too.

*Psalms.*

Even the sparrow finds a home and the swallow a nest.

*Proverbs.*

Like a sparrow in its flitting, like a swallow in its flying, an undeserved curse goes nowhere.

Oh how he misses those days, in the green unconfined hills; and fishing in the Tywi. *The Tawe*, as his father taught him, poshing him up. One day that son would sedate an aristocrat, mind, and *there's posh*.

Down the corridors of the asylum echoes a turbulent commotion and alarms fly. This was the bit the staff heard. With our song, we held a beautiful rebellion on the way to bed and we trilled, into the past, to Blanche and Bertha, to the present and to others and ourselves of the future: Women untie your voices—look up and out!

Then, our carers, some fine, some tardy or tristy, heard us. But oh, they'd missed the whispers, glissando of the winged helpers no louder than a heartbeat through a greatcoat; rustles

40

of paper and scratches of soft pencil. A tremendous thing. Nothing could stop it now.

That night Violet whispered to me, before they locked the doors and mopped us down with sedatives, hypnotics and the like— and she said: You've got a hell of a story to get down tomorrow, dear girl. Clarify your thought as best you can. Get some rest.

And I suppose I need to remind you, reader, of something because you might, depending on your provenance, ask whether what happens next really does happen. What, even, of some of the previous? True? Did you too feel your cheek caressed by the wings of birds when it was our bedtime? You are going, I think, to be asking a *how*. Well, we are not time travellers and this is not science fiction. Violet is not the author of *The Chrysalids* or *Earthlight*—and in case you are wondering, these are titles from last year, 1955, sitting dusty in a corner of the day room here. We both glanced at them, Violet spat them out. No, as I was saying. How does it happen? Well remember what I had written down earlier. That Violet tells of such things and people; mad women of the past. Talks about them as if she knows them and says she can, through thirty years of rattling through her tale and their tale and reading about them—I told you: she reads everything!—well, says she can drum up these women. She's researched; she's rehearsed. Voices of mad women junked up to dance for men at the Salpêtrière in Paris. Humiliated in myriad ways. And there's your answer. She's had time, and her desire to remember lost women and to have an adventure are urgent; so too her wish to help me. And whatever adventure she has, whatever she says, I, my dears, will be entering fully into it too.

I have made a decision. I am going to aid and abet and I cannot wait!

Only this. If I ask you whether any of this really happened, later on, I mean, I don't want you to be sure and, reader, I want your answer to rest on a generous ambiguity. Because I'd argue that life—and sanity—do, too.

# 4

We have escaped like a bird from the snare of the fowlers; the
snare is broken and we have escaped!

Psalm 124.

This is the story of the robin.

Violet pictured her in this way. Plump, inquisitive little
bird. Yes, it is Blanche's story; she was a hysteric, Violet told
me, at the enormous hospital in Paris, in the late nineteenth
and early twentieth century. Blanche, Violet says, was born
eighteen years, or thereabouts, before her; she died when I,
Lucia, was six. I wonder if, as I grew and knew Paris, I had
heard of her. Did I even see her? Because of the muddling
things that have happened to me, there are memories which
erupt and in which I swim, but of their veracity I cannot always
be sure, though I've come to wonder if that matters so much.
You know—that empirical truth. Yes, Blanche. Sometimes,
it may have been that she lived, died or was buried not far
away from us, the Joyces, in Paris, when we were there. She
was famous, too, as a sort of glamorous defective. Violet
said it made her mad as hell, the way Blanche got painted:
blouse glossy and voluminous, like a gorgeous thing, but that
she'd set this to rights so we could hear her voice too. And
I remembered: somewhere in Paris I saw a little copy of this
painting of this fine woman, Blanche, on display, and even
then I understood, in myself, the anger that would be nursed
by Violet. There she was, *so* pretty, buxom and velveteen, not

all skew-eyed and jutting jaw like me. But she was not free: she was a subject and she was an object.

These memories. They tugged at me as Violet began to tell me Blanche's story, as she understood it. And I began to write it all down as Violet spoke. I could not believe what came out of her mouth, how full and real a story—but, like I said, those who are confined have the best imaginations. Thus it was as if Blanche were suddenly vibrantly in the room and Violet, auteur, began the story of The Queen of the Hysterics. Someone else to take on this adventure that Violet had conceived. Someone to save and liberate.

The Salpêtrière

Paris,

1887.

Here I am! exhales Blanche.

Oh, I should add that Blanche speaks in French, so this is the translation. I speak all kinds from my raggedy exotic childhood. It was that exotic, sometimes we sat round a big pot gnawing on chicken bones, like savages, in a borrowed apartment, on borrowed time, and on raggedy hessian lay. Violet's French is good, too, but it's a little too polished, too small a vernacular, so I've done my best, with a plain speaking miraculous girl. I've helped Violet along.

And Violet speaks, in French, as Blanche, for Blanche, and it is irresistible:

When I was a child I heard a story about Cock Robin. A song, or a poem? It frightened me. Stuck and echoed. It was creepy and dark, but it had a sort of order and even then I sensed it was important to me, but how I could not express. I loved little birds, songbirds. And I remembered it, the whole thing.

Who killed Cock Robin?

I, said the Sparrow, with my bow and arrow,

I killed Cock Robin.

Who saw him die?

I, said the Fly, with my little eye!

It goes on, this strange ditty. Sometimes I wish I could not remember it, but you see my days, when I am not required to perform, are filled with a head world. Memories; snatches of song and poem.

Who'll dig his grave?

I, said the Owl, with my little trowel,

I'll dig his grave.

Who'll be the parson?

I, said the Rook, with my little book.

Who would mourn for me and where should I be buried? I'll not have a stone, with a carving. Women like me, well, we don't, do we?

Who'll carry the coffin?

I, said the Kite, if it's not through the night,

I'll carry the coffin.

Was it made by my mad father? Out in his workshop, he turned them out and, when he was drunk and his loathing for me too great, he'd bang me up in one. Only coffin I'll ever have! Women like us, now we have our brains examined downstairs, sliced and diced. To see what stains insanity and in particular hysteria has planted on this miraculous organ. Once we are dead I mean! Ha! Then off we go in the wagon and into the communal pit. That's what I heard. But this odd little story.

All the birds of the air fell a-sighing and a-sobbing,

when they heard the bell toll for poor Cock Robin.

Yes, I'd like to think I'd be mourned and that a song thrush would sing for me.

Do you know that there is a different ending, yes? The sparrow who killed Cock Robin is hanged for what he has done. A sparrow is a pretty round bird, stripe and mottles, but here a villain and he is not ashamed and the birds of the air, they see him kill and yet he is not ashamed. Justice is done and not; it is not pretty. Sometimes, at night, I would cry for both the birds. For the dead bird and for the monster who was not sorry. And,

I suppose, for all the dead and wasted. For the eight thousand *femmes en colère* at the Salpêtrière hospital.

Sometimes I thought too long and hard and I woke, eyes wet, into the cruel draught at the window, above the furriers where I worked, and I knew I had been dreaming about my family, long gone; my father, at the asylum, held and stilled into the night. I did not yet know what was to come, what brutality.

You know, he was a showman in a dark felt coat. He loved to drip with acclaim; it wasn't all for the ready health of our minds when he said: Come in, come in!

He was Charcot. One of the world's greatest doctors. I hear them talk. A neurologist who mapped a continent; a stubborn observer of the brains in the corpses downstairs, too. But I hear them say he doesn't always find what he is looking for.

They said, the whispering spectators, that my breast was milk white when my loose shirts fetched up and I fell, under his power as he compressed and spoke of what I suffered. But I was not his lover. That was whispered alright, but I am no-one's lover. I have given too much already and there is no more. Not yet.

And Charcot, pacing the floor for pitch and build-up, slows to a halt and begins to declaim:

This, ladies and gentleman, is *hysteria*.

This is Blanche, a willing subject for you today!

She has fallen under the hypnotism and you see, ladies and gentleman, what I see, but not so much, not so much: so let me explain. She cannot tell her story, so let me, as I teach and as you learn. It is a marvel. Attend!

Monsieur Brouillet came to paint me; I was quite the thing against the stygian black of the doctors, don't you think? The tendrils of my hair escaping down my neck. I had poise and gravitas in the picture. Brouillet did not paint the days I crawled and slavered like a dog from *la grande hystérie*, although, somewhere in Charcot's offices, there are thick folders of photographs of the others; of us: prone; upright; startled;

reclining: teeth bared; *down, girl.* His, his spectators: come the night, to their salon they went: artists, doctors, le tout Paris, and back I went: locked up, of course. In my imagination, though, I flew, sang like a nightingale and my song flew out from the window, *jug jug.* In society, though: absinthe, done prettily, that is, and lovely crystal; the tinkling piano, and the sweet savoury smell of pâté and pes.

Here, stew. Boiled to destruction. And grey blankets, boiled up. For the lice—because we were legion.

There were other women, but I was the best. Marie, I was the queen of the hysterics, except, of course, he made my name Blanche and I was milky white, my breast milky white, as I said, as he compressed and as he showed me to his distinguished guests. He hypnotised me; these moments I don't remember, but it is said I was a fine thing. I must be fair: people wanted to know, did they not? Interest was high and he sought to teach. Galen; Hippocrates, the Greeks saw hysteria in women and thus was born the wandering womb, cause of hysteria.

Aretaeus, he wrote on the subject: I learned about it, though I could not read, because here in the hospital, beside the whores and the beggars, there were clever women, who knew about all science, about books and journals. Clever women who had been forbidden by their men from knowing about all kinds, so why do you suppose they were here? I should add that there were also clever whores and clever beggars! But as I was saying, I learned about Aretaeus because I was trying to understand what he, Charcot, had read, so: In the middle of the flanks of women lies the womb, a female viscus, closely resembling an animal; for it is moved of itself hither and thither in the flanks, also upwards in a direct line to below the cartilage of the thorax, and also obliquely to the right or to the left, either to the liver or the spleen, and it likewise is subject to prolapsus downwards, and in a word, it is altogether erratic. It delights also in fragrant smells, and advances towards them; and it has an aversion to foetid smells,

46

and flees from them; and, on the whole, the womb is like an animal within an animal.

And what do you think about all *that*?

Dear Charcot, do you know, Charcot, do you know know— *no*? I knew about the bodies and brains, downstairs. He would look and look to see what he could find, what illness there. If not a wandering womb, if not now days of Galen's humours all awry, what then? Such skill in pathology and all he had to do was wait. Not that we died from madness; it's just they, his women, eight thousand, never left, gasped their last in the sallow corridors of this place. He thought we might be cured; those who could dance, under his magic, showman. He was dedicated; I think that he was kind. Famous neurologist, he could have gone anywhere. Instead, he stayed here, on and on, watched and watching: Freud, he came, the young Janet: I watched them all. And *le tout Paris*, just to see the show. Hysteria grew and grew, under his hands. Do you suppose that he had created it? I worry that I helped. Made madness into a show and circus or made hysteria become, forgive me, more hysterical. When he died, it stopped because I did not think of it anymore and, obviously, neither did he.

I came to the Salpêtrière as a nurse and my life had been hard. I had seen madness cage up my father and then he saw me not. Mother was gone. My siblings, too. The world pressed in on me and language failed and when I tried, it flooded out in jags and rags and it was no good and it hurt: I stopped talking. Outside my window, I saw the songbirds skittering against the jalousies and a whisper from the future said *Fly*!

Then. One morning, as I woke, I was cold and hard in bed. I often cried, as I said, into the cold night of my room. This time it was different. I felt palsy in my face; what smile I tried to make at the new day, it fought with me and my lip quivered and dropped pathetically. I felt the slobber on my pillow and I was ashamed, though there was no-one to see. And sometimes they saw me rotten and convulsed. I don't remember how, each

47

time, it started, but I would wake, I thought, in a road, on a grey pavement, sometimes streaked with blood, and they said, *she is mad, she is mad.* But all I felt was this: the great granite block of sadness and it would not, before I woke, before I slept, ever dislodge. And Charcot saw me in a new way and he took notice of me and I was changed and I was patient not nurse, this time, and so it began.

Charcot. One of the most famous doctors in the world and he could look at you alive or dead; he had the skills of intricacy. Downstairs, he would look at the brains of those who had died mad, seeking the signs of damage caused by the hysteric's excess of imagination. It was said that he did not find what he was looking for. The ischaemic (I heard him use that word: it was quite new, apparently) jags and lines of ageing and of a life ill-lived, perhaps, but nothing more. Yet still he was convinced. For such maladies, for the hysterics, he would and must find an organic cause. He *would.* Neurology: such detail—and he swam in its glory and down its pathways; he thought hysteria had a logic of the body.

Hmmm.

I don't recall that he studied it in men, did he? I saw no scabrous man swoon and fall to the floor in the hospital salon. No loon was jabbed or pressed there and I don't think he imported any males for, you know, the downstairs room where he was, so I overheard, to look for lesions on their dead but once-overheated brains!

Oh, Monsieur had poise and beauty in his beautiful embroidered felt coat. In my head, my father would say, *Oh Monsieur Charcot, he is so clever and so elegant! His demonstrations are the talk of Paris!*—as if we were part of any society that mattered—but Father, he... Father was elsewhere. I do not know how they held him, at his worst, in his madness, and I did not see. Still it was torture to me. He was not a good man, as such, but I was not without feelings for him, so I would wake in the hospital and wonder where he was confined: if

48

he were dead, or alive, but in a living death in an asylum. At ours, the Salpêtrière, Charcot noticed me; in my world, things changed: I made the road from nurse to patient. Then, I was interesting; I inhaled, he pressed magnets upon me, compressed on my ovaries and it was not delicate and then the hypnosis. *And oh! I was good*. I was spectacular, in fact. Madness can be so tender, the erotic tempting you to look, when your sense of shame, your tidy sense of decorum says, *no: you should not*.

You have seen the Brouillet painting of me, as I fall back, louche and beautiful? There were doctors there, as perhaps you realised? Students, but also the great and good of Paris society and, after I had performed, a party at his house. Piano; crème de menthe; a world I did not know but which I scented.

What did I know, and what had I known? I wonder if, in years to come, ideas and imaginings will be written down as facts and what I did not intend or become will be transfigured into untruth. That could happen to someone like me. I think this: I am unknown and yet, I am painted and seen and exhibited to many, many. Charcot's lover! Look how she responds to his touch and his press upon her. I was special, you see. I knew about Augustine, Queen of the Hysterics before me. Some said she could see only in black and white; this was her curious affliction and her histrionics were exceptional. There were whispers that she was his favourite, or his lover, but only that. Whispers went all day and all night! And as for black and white, well now, that I had seen, from time to time, because sometimes all the colour was drained from the world for I was alone, though observed. And if Augustine were here, if she had not gone out, escaped as she did in the garb of a man, I think she would understand me.

When I was a little girl, and Father was mad, he would take me to his workshop where he made the coffins and he would shut me up in one to punish me and I would hear him laugh and cry and beat his head. Then it was black, inside. Like death, as you would expect; Father did not use thin splints but only made the best because he had standards. And when I came out, breathless, soiled, the light was white and nothing else. Upstairs was Mother, nervous attack, not interceding; we were nine, then we were four, consumptive, dirty, but survived. I was the eldest, sometimes their mother. Too much. When he raged, Father put me in the coffin again: I saw in black and white, like Augustine, and I felt that everything I had ever held in my hand fell down. For whom could I care, and who would protect me? I broke, I think, I broke: and Charcot: he was not a bad man. People whispered, from outside, tens of thousands maybe, that it was show and mimicry—but he believed. He just had not found the cause. I think.

Think.

Think.

*Think, Blanche!* It's all mine, what's in there; in my mind.

I think that there is a place in the body where sorrow must come out; that our minds cannot bear it all and it must have recourse. Tears. My whole life shook, it made no sense. He, Charcot, tried to make sense of what it was, and for that I accord him thanks.

Later, Dr Janet, who had been, I think, Charcot's most prized student, wrote that my left eye showed complete achromatopsia. I could see no colours, except for saturated red. Yes, and for a while: black and white, like Augustine. Augustine? Remember? It might be important. Hysteric, escaped, dressed as a man, so the story goes. She was my predecessor as Queen of the Hysterics and my friend. Every night, I wonder where she is and what she is. What is her identity now? Does she live among men? Is she pretty, as she was here, or a pretty man? Suited, booted, confident because she tastes a glorious freedom. The windows here are small, but what if those were her feet, running rat-a-tat past me? She runs, in her man suit; she's so tired of being a pretty girl but never, never, will she tire of running. No-one runs at the Salpêtrière, apart from to get away from a needle, or to restrain one of the mads and then they come with the tough white jacket, arms down dear, nothing to be done: *camisole de force*. *Camisole*; sounds almost pretty.

Oh yes: the achromatopsia. I could see only black and white. And saturated red. Or rather Dr Janet, while Charcot nodded assent, explained to others that this is what I could see. I heard him! Certainly, I had seen and sensed things I should not. Such as horrors here, even though it is not, so we hear on the wing, the worst of these places. So. That must have been why the brutal splash of carmine on black and white. Yes. Here I had seen things I should not. In the outside world, too

Epileptid.

Clonic.

Then Delirium.

That was it; me, summed up.

Charcot pressed gold upon me, I am told I swallowed metals—he believed all this—pressed down upon my ovaries, the hysterogenic zones: he blew on my eyes to wake me from this time. I was calm, but exhausted. Afterwards, I lay on my bed, rough sheets and blankets, but clean as they could. My stomach was tender and I felt there; kneaded it with my knuckles and, finding it too tender, lifted my shirts and saw my name blazoned there by a pin. I asked Charcot, although he did not say so much. Not branding, or joke, but observation of an erythemic band, noting how raised my skin would become, calibrating it against hysteria and the health of my nerves, my organs.

He'd scratched my name on my flesh with a pin.

Gilbert Ballet wrote about me—he is there in the painting by Brouillet, you know. The side group by the inner window; he adored Charcot and he was handsome! A well-thought-of man; a doctor whose nascent skill they spoke of. At our salon. I winked at him, between acts, and startled the poor ingénue. Dr Ballet made his *Blanche* case notes: apparently, I had a hallucination, a phantasy of a bird. I saw it and caressed it. Sometimes I glimpsed it, *coup d'oeil*! Then, oh it disappeared. And Charcot used metallotherapy. The gold—and I was superbly responsive

51

to copper, too. When he swung the little discs, the bird moved, shifted, flew away; was disappeared. And Charcot tried again. Magnets; forks; electrical currents: aesthesiogens, Charcot called them. I always listened to him, when I could, sane enough: he believed that he could direct the fall of symptoms from one part of my body to another, hands caressing me like the wings of a bird. He believed he was finding tremendous therapeutic things. As I said, he was a great man, the things he found to the good but here... I am not sure. After all, I never left the Pitié-Salpêtrière.

Recovery. That last bit of the doctor's list, I added; the others were my, our stages, witness the notes. My opinion was that I recovered from whatever it was, but here I stayed.

As I was saying.

I was spectacular, a fine thing, under hypnosis. I convulsed, I calmed, rattled and shook and at each cue, I was just so. No longer plain Marie, but *Blanche*; after a while, only my stage name was known. It was not a trick. I thought, *In years to come, what will they think of this? Am I a gimcrack show; a performer? What, then, will they know about the workings of our minds and bodies?*

Oh, but I knew I held the title now: Queen of the Hysterics. And although Monsieur Charcot had others, showy demonstrators, I outclassed them all. Here, he would say, is a picture of you *deshabillée*, my dear. Shall we show it to the assembled company? and of course I would roar and in my flagrant modesty, I would snatch up the picture and tear it. Later, he would be saying: But it was just a blank piece of paper, so you see, so you see! Suggestible in the extreme, my friends. *That* is how hysteria is.

There were other times.

Poison in a little vial.

*Give it to that gentleman, Blanche, do it now please.*

I would go, as directed, to poison him.

And afterwards, I would hear him say: But just a vial of water. So you see, so you see.

In my notes I am told (how do they see and how is this news passed on? We are clever: we distract and then we whisper what we have found out) it said that my skin was white and that I was blonde and of a lymphatic complexion and that my bosom was very large... Just a thought, but my forehead is large, too and I gather that *this* suggests intelligence.

Charcot, as I said, such a famous doctor. Brilliant as a pathologist, or when travelling the nerves, but missing, missing always, as I later heard. But when I was Blanche they came in troupes to him; if you wanted to study nerves and medicine, then sit at his feet. He looked and looked and did not speak. As a nurse, I saw them, the patients, come to his office, where he would receive them, not on the ward. He did not touch or palpate, but looked and looked and said little—oh but did he *see?* When Augustine escaped in her man suit, they did not see *that*, did they? I'm imagining now that this wonderful girl flew in circles round Sacré-Cœur; she could not have been more obvious! Ah. You were paying attention. You queried and I am proud of you. Sacré-Cœur had not been built yet. Still. We learn to be imaginative, when we are caged. And when I hear words, be sure that I will remember them. Now, *you* remember *that*.

There was a man, I heard in whispers, who came and studied and wondered. Freud. Going to be a great one, I heard. He saw me. Did he admire me—Queen? It is not for me to say. I understood, in these whispers, that he saw what I had become as of the mind; that was my pathology: a sick mind. I would have liked to know more of what he said, for I do not want you to think that I... that I put it on; that I acted. But my body was strong, then, I secretly thought; at night my pain came up from secret seas and drowned me and I was Marie, death and the maiden, and Father bound over, stilled, contained, in the asylum. He'd been a brute to me. As I told you, he was not a good man, but I had feelings for him and the pain of waking at night, wondering if he were dead or dead, alive, in an asylum, now it was eviscerating. *There* is a horrid word I like.

53

Charcot. In his embroidered coat. He was resplendent, confident, but as he watched me, so I watched him and I felt him strange; saw that confidence begin to falter. He was a great man; the years will tell you that. And he believed in art and in keeping records, so the photographs went on for miles: women with mouths wide as boats, agog, hands splayed, rictus-backed. Shrieking and falling back happy and then terrified of Hell.

Once I thought I heard him cry, but then there were many tears, how could I so distinguish? There were eight thousand at the Salpêtrière.

Tears. Oceans of them. Some of them his.

I was the hysteric until a death: his, not mine. Came a man, Dr Janet. *The next man.* I heard he told the world so much more about the mind, about the ills it caused in the body. Was that how it was? I doubted myself. I did not convulse again. I stayed in the Salpêtrière, because where else would I go? Some thought I would never recover. But I did, I did. That's why I added it to the narrative, earlier.

Do you have a narrative I can follow? One you think fitting for me?

Here is one story that was put about and repeated. A story circulated of work and purpose: you know who I was with, then, when hysteria had gone off? When people hear this story, they cannot believe it; I was invaluable to her. *The great Madame Curie*, who worked in her laboratory near our asylum! You would say I paid for my work, hobbled appallingly as I was by the radium, but I had purpose. Then I was Madame Curie's confidante and the pitchblende we worked with gave me vast lesions, took my legs and my left arm. But I was not a symbol, not a torso with a tired head and a wooden trolley: I was me and I was complete. All my questions in my little coloured books that I will leave, one day, to be discovered!

No.

Are you observing carefully? I was saying *it was a story. Fiction at play.* Attend! I was whole; injured by radium, working in the little lab at the Salpêtrière, yes, and the lesions were intolerable, but I was used to intolerable and I was whole—and I could sway and dance.

There is so much more to me than meets the eye: everywhere I went, I thought, I noted. The notebooks. I've been hearing I kept them, with lots of detail of Madame Curie, her loves and work. My loves and questions to the universe and Venus Aphrodite? No; they were not real. I confined my words to letters I thought I might send—but to whom?—when I could. Where are they now? And after all those years, I could barely write or read, so you might think a child wrote them. But still they existed. Everything else is the narrative you made for me and not my own legend. The one you accepted for me, not I.

There are stories, wrong, desolate, all over the world. And I think there are unsent letters all over the world. Letters of mad women. True, desolate.

I think there are unvisited graves and burials not as were wanted.

How might a letter begin? Dearest love, do you miss me? Are you coming for me? Come soon. I do not like it here and I am walled up and frightened.

*Records file in the cabinet, nurse.*

Please listen, my darling. I should like a Catholic burial, full rites and only Catholics present. A simple stone but with a meaningful inscription and scripture about liberty. *We have escaped like a bird from the snare of the fowlers; the snare is broken, and we have escaped.* Or, *Under his wings you shall find refuge.*

At this, I, Lucia, made Violet break off with the story and I said: Violet, I think that this is your burial wish and your desire for freedom and refuge that you are describing. And she said: There you have me, Lucy Light. I am in the company of such sympathetic women, my deepest wants are unfettered. And you'll remember, won't you? About my death and what to do?

So I nodded and she continued so that Blanche could tell us more of those forgotten women, crying behind bars, placed there, often, by their menfolk.

Please dear, remember my funeral wants? The things we spoke about together, before you felt the need to bring me here. I know: I was sharp and difficult and my quarrels were difficult for you; my rage radical and showing I was losing control of my thought, becoming, even, insensate. You asked what else you could have done. Said it was for my own good. Yes, yes, yes, you would visit me, when you could. You would come. To the Salpêtrière, as other husbands you knew visited; took the trip out to Bicêtre and to the other hospitals in the towns and provinces of France. I do know it was worse, far worse, for women who came before me, oh yes. The days of keeping us in chains was over. I don't mean to be ungrateful. It is said that here, at the Salpêtrière, they choose the attendants with such care! Oh, I think I can tell who's good at their job. I wonder, too, if Charcot thinks I have made particularly interesting photographs, when I am at my most... excessive? But you'll come, won't you? I shan't be here forever. Oh no, I can tell that I am improving!

*Delusions. Poor old thing. Yes, delusions of grandeur, alright. Scratch that. She won't know and it's not as if she'll get visitors!*

Please. Husband? Why am I here? Everyone watches me and I can find no peace. I cannot always get things into words, and I tense from being watched, so I draw. Eyes, again and again. That is what it feels like inside my head, inside my body. Please bring me home!

*File. She's drawing eyes again. They are just phantasms; delusions. Poor old thing.*

Now Violet speaks only for herself, telling of the campaigns she has planned and the pressure she has, for years, tried to exert: she wants to get out and to go home.

Dear Sir, I beg you to consider my petition. This was to a Prime Minister. I am not so sure why I said these two things, though they came easily to me.

*Just tear that up altogether. She's written hundreds, the same.*
When I die, I would like a proper Mass said...
*Ha. Nice try, sweetheart.*
I keep my things safe.
*File*: inside mattress cover.
And when I die? Nobody knows where I am going then.
*File:* be still, my heart.
And now Violet takes up the story of Blanche, Queen of the Hysterics, once more.

I have to tell you that there is so much more to know, for all my life I have been a student and there is nothing that I did not note from the quiet corner of my eye when the world thought I was not looking. I was Marie Wittmann, not Blanche, but I think my stage name suits me better! Remember me as you will, but remember me. Perhaps as a songbird, of true flight and piercing song, with a white ruffle at my throat and plumage orderly, limning the sky, just so. Or a robin, plump and pretty and so very alive. I cannot go out, but my thoughts cannot be caged. I am not even sure that Marie was my name, but a name I heard. What do you think? But I know I am not Blanche. Not wholly. And I am not only a specimen, a case.

The nurse said there was a letter for me, but who would write? My siblings ran; Mother and Father, well...

They cannot have looked closely at this impossible thing. Its date; the stamps! Cockerel, emblem of the French Republic; that was right; my century; my year: but another. I rubbed my eyes, laughing. Hysterical! But no, it was there. *From England*, said the postmark; *1956* stamped as its date. A pretty queen, cobalt blue, thistles, sceptre, a bird. All this I could read.

But how is this letter possible? Generations and seas away.
What do you know what is possible, who has not been mad?
Who'll sing a psalm?
I, said the Thrush, as she sat on a bush, I'll sing a psalm.
Even the sparrow finds a home and the swallow a nest.
What?—

These things: they keep coming to me. Like a prompt, or a conversation I started once with a dear friend. Or a momentary insight in childhood, that opened up a door.

Violet rested back on her pillow, and the voice of Blanche ended on the most delicate note of—was it?—uplift and hope. Violet smiled at me, though she was exhausted. She was lying in her bed, back, for her last days, in a better room of her own, not in the communal ward downstairs to which the family had transferred her to save money, with some help from the National Health Service, just eight years old at this point. Yes, the private room was much better for listening and scribing. From this upper floor, we could see birds skittering across the sky and were more aware of the moods of light, in the natural world, beyond. In its way, it was peaceful. My room was near hers. I was glad of that at night, at the worst times. But whether in the day or at night, in a room of one's own or on the ward with the other feebles, Violet had read and thought about other women, penned up and mistranslated, or just forgotten for who they might really have been. She saw them, she said, in her dreams, too, and at all times, heard their voices and mouthed them aloud; answered back, saving it all in her imagination, which had grown expansive, luxuriant, in confinement.

Tell me, I said, of the other—of the other fine lady you wanted me to know.

She closed her eyes, said: Tomorrow. And slept.

# 5

Darkling I listen; and, for many a time,
I have been half in love with easeful Death...

Keats, *Ode to a Nightingale*

The nightingale. Bertha's story, who was Anna O.

It is Vienna. 1882 and we will see, Violet tells me, the office and clinic of Dr Breuer, who treats her there, then at Bertha's home, accompanied. They also send someone to watch her. You'll want to know who she was, then who she is. She was a famous patient, examined and put in a book, while Blanche got photographed with the myriad hysterics and painted by Brouillet. Did either consent to such publicity?

Now, I have been learning. As I told you, what I did not gain from Violet, I found out. At St Andrew's they were kind enough not to show restraint on reading material.

For years, until after her death in 1936, you would not have known the identity of one Anna O, though she was studied by Dr Breuer and taken up by Freud; though she has a foothold, because of her intelligence and her derangement, in the very history of psychiatry and of women like us. But just recently, who she was has come to light. Yes, 1953, a biography of Freud which Violet showed me; she's been reading it, although she says he's deadly, Freud. Ghastly. Irreligious. All that regarding-God-as-an-illusion malarkey, our thirst for Him being part of an infantile need for a powerful father figure. Violet finds that offensive. Says she prays because it pours out of her. It is painful for her to believe in God and she aches when she speaks to Mary, but it is a necessity and inescapable, lawful as breathing. Real. And besides which, she says, Freud *would* say that, wouldn't he?

I am sorry, Violet is so very entertaining, so clever, she makes me digress! The book about Freud: it revealed that Anna O was Bertha Pappenheim, a Jewish social worker—founder of fine things, creator of a home, Neu-Isenburg, for young Jewish women and their babies, their children—educator. I think she was a ball of kindness and duty.

Bertha died when I, Lucia Anna, was twenty-nine and, again, memory tugs at me. I was not well then, not always. That was 1936, as I said, and we were in Zurich; Daddy had consented to my treatment under Jung—*call me Carl, dear, or Gustav*—and shortly before this I had been diagnosed with schizophrenia at the Burghölzli clinic. I felt my body tremulous; felt the strings were false. What I thought, I could not communicate, so dark it was. But I was not convinced by what they said, the specialists. Over the years, I overheard so many things of what was wrong with me, what was not. Doctors could not agree.

In 1936, Violet had been here, at St Andrew's, nearly ten years. And Daddy, though he swore to the barnacle (sorry, my mother. Did I explain this already? Well I shan't recant!) that he would never have me incarcerated among the English, well he sent me here, to St Andrew's, for blood tests. Yes, here. Sedated, sleepy, day and night eliding, I came to this place before and I thought... as we entered... I thought I saw her, then. On the way to a corner of the day room, or the dining room, watched by a nurse: a tiny figure, ancient-seeming, but immaculate in her black crêpe dress. The Honourable Violet Albina Gibson. I did not know I would come back. My father had heard of her, the would-be assassin of Mussolini. I heard him talking about the hospital's infamous inmate. Now, *there* would have been a book for him.

Little did I know!

They could not—I heard them talking to my father on the telephone: it could even have been Dr Griffith. In fact, it must have been—keep me here, after my blood tests, for very long because I wanted out. *No, Mr Joyce, we do understand your concern, but Miss Joyce would like to leave now and we are not obliged to insist she stay. Yes, Mr Joyce, that is the case and we have done all we can and please reassure Mrs Joyce of this.* I had a sense of home being elsewhere, then. Perhaps home was just with him.

And Daddy, as I said, told them again, *Quite, but no: I will not have her incarcerated among the English* and back to Paris I went. I stayed in Neuilly sur Seine, with Maria Jolas, wife of my father's literary friend, Eugene Jolas. Oh, she was a remarkable woman, strong and brave; from Kentucky, that was it! I thought, in this pretty place, I could strengthen, but I felt myself sink and it was frightening. I screamed and then I remember the straitjacket, the *camisole de force,* as we say. At Vésinet they kept me in isolation; said I was a danger. I rocked shut.

Have you the faintest notion what such separation, such schism, can do to you? There, I sat all day, isolated for two months, howling, raging and nursing images; trying to build a storied imagination so that I could survive. I think this is what Violet has done too. War came, I heard. Then I was shuffled off to the hospital of Dr Delmas at Ivry-sur-Seine. He kept us safe (and here is another story) from the Nazis; such feebles to experiment on. I don't know how he kept us safe, but he did.

Mother did not come.

Then Daddy was dead. 1941. I heard on my little radio, at Ivry. I could have rotted away there, never met Violet. They would have left me. But there were friends, you know. And they called me here, to you, to England, and to *you,* Lady Gibson. From France, in the end, to my forever home (though Violet says I should not think of it in those terms, not any more). What with the new world she has in store for me and all.

I did not mean to talk so much about myself. I am trying to show you who and what I am, as far as I know. And I've come to see the little threads that bind me to Violet, through time, and to other women who were also desperately ill but madly, madly sane.

And so I say to Violet that I am tired of talking about myself and she says: Well, yes, you have been running on rather a lot, dear girl! Also that it is time to tell of Anna O, who was really Bertha Pappenheim and who had, in our time together at St Andrew's, just been revealed to the world for who she was—and what she was was remarkable, of course. But oh, the sorrow. I learned that Bertha never fully got better and that her loss was prolific. And Violet began:

They called me Anna O, but the O is oblique, hinting at a glamour and a mystery I might despise, or hiding me. I did not choose it and I will not take it with me: I refuse.

Now, history will tell you that, amongst other things, I am a fine case study and, if you were to look me up, you should see that I am most closely associated with the Austrian psycho-analyst, Sigmund Freud. I am in his book, with Dr Josef Breuer. It is called *Studies in Hysteria*. How do I know that? Oh, we shall see, we shall see! But then I took my stage name, Anna O, in which I had no say; it was not my book. I did not meet him, Freud. I saw him, I would say, in passing, but it was with Dr Breuer that I worked and so, at first, you came to know me. I became important, though not, as it turned out, as myself, because Dr Breuer relayed my case to Freud and the rest is history.

Anna O.

O.

Oh!

The name: do you want to know, do you? A little bird told me that not until I was dead nineteen years would the world know the other self. It's true. In all my work, in all my years, I never breathed a word, although I went back and back again, for help, to make me better. I was not ashamed, but I feared the world would shame me, as it does its mad women. In all my time, in the home I built for those in need, as Bertha Pappenheim, I would not let the doctors come for these kinds of talking cures for the girls we looked after. We listened, nursed and supported, but *Leave them to our care,* said I. They meant well you see, just as Freud, after Breuer, but I was not convinced. He might have thought, Dr Freud, that I was the spark, the flower, the I-don't-know-what of his psychoanalysis, and the methods worked, but yet I was ill, again and again. I did not, as these doctors might have thought, get fully well. Yet I did not give up: I had purpose and there was work, so much work, to be done.

Oh yes, the name. Do you want to know? A comes before B for Bertha and O comes before P for Pappenheim. I suppose it's a sort of code, but it's not a hard one, is it?

What do you want to know and what do you expect? My parents were good, I had a brother and two sisters; we adhered to Orthodox Judaism and we had a pretty little silver cat. Does this sum up my early years for you? I read my Torah; I thought, prayed and observed and I was clever; not that I said so aloud, but it was just that I watched from the window as a counterpane of gorgeous colours began to unfold; there it went. So much to see. Smiles; a look that meant a world, a history; poetry, the man who walked past every morning, quietly narrating the story of his life because he had nowhere else to tell it. I decided, for this lonely lonely man, that I would tell a story, one day.

Always, I felt the compulsion to tell a tale and do you know, when Dr Breuer helped me, it was often with the beginning of a story to help me speak, to communicate my distress and see its seed—and he gave each line the same tone, same words: he said *There was a boy...* and I continued. I told the story of this man I mentioned, as the boy, but made his story different where he was surrounded by love and friends to support him and let his imagination and his wants fly free. I said: There was a boy who was lonely, playing with his hoop and ball but he found someone to tell and, as he grew up, his wits got sharper and more confident and he understood who to trust and, though his world was not safe, he had friends and confidants and so he was a fine man, confidence and bearing. And I said that if his confidence became brimming too much with pride, then he could become like the hoopoe in the stories of my faith, full of judgement: judgement and bearing. But then I wasn't thinking of the sad boy who became a sad man, against the gorgeous colours of the world. I was thinking of these eminent folk, these doctors. I've heard other stories: they think they know it all! That they are indispensable. I'd say they are, at best, a conduit to better health.

Yes, he made me begin my stories with *THERE WAS A BOY*.

And really, sometimes I was thinking *THERE WAS A GIRL. A GIRL.*

There was me and I know there are others, silenced and chastened. It is not right.

But as I was saying!

Dr Breuer had me *perfekt* in his notes: who I was and what was happening. I had stages and my first was *Latent Incubation*.

But as I was saying! Make yourself clear Bertha, to keep your narrative before it's stolen.

*THERE WAS A GIRL!*

Henriette, sister, dead at eight from tuberculosis and so it began; things shifted and I became aware. Death; judgement; last things; eschatology, not that this was a word I knew as a girl, but I knew I was clever and I glimpsed what was in store. It was the time it was. My schooling did not last long, but I learned to sew and it was as much leisure as labour, but I never got over that first harsh death, with the rasps of sour breath and the clear eyes of my sister and Mother's drear cries.

So.

Anna O.

64

My father, 1880, a year of bed and washing him; lifting his head and feeling disgusted by, though ashamed to say so, the tart breath of the dying..

Going. Gone.

There came a morning, 1881. I was ill, stiff necked, dizzy and confused; sneezing, scant of breath, confused and mourning. Then, in grief and so lonely, I was frightened and I went to see Dr Breuer. I was unsure, then.

Caring took a toll on me. At one point, they would not let me see Father. I was too weak.

*Manifest illness* wrote Dr Breuer in his notes.

It stung; I had cared; I was exhausted; it was meant well, but to have failed him was death, judgement: the last... I forget the rest of the sentence.

I've read the notes. How? They don't notice everything, these experts. Freud said I lived a healthy, active life; liked to daydream; good in the house; devoted. He said that Dr Breuer's patient was a girl of twenty-one, of high intellectual gifts. Her illness lasted for over two years, and she developed a series of physical and psychological disturbances; oh yes—the tics and tremors moved around my body and then I suffered from a rigid paralysis, accompanied by loss of sensation, like a muting I would describe it, of both extremities on the right side of my body; and the same trouble from time to time affected me on my left side. Dr Freud said that *the girl's* movements—and remember THERE WAS A GIRL!—were disturbed and her sight was restricted. Oh! But all the time I fought it. It was sight blindness; my inner eye was penetrating, but I did not have recourse to tell of what it saw. This was not in his notes. He said I, the girl, had an aversion to taking nourishment, but that was not quite it; inside I raged and fought to say I was hungry and thirsty: I called to the birds of the air. I said *Come to me, beautiful passerines!* that exquisite word, so poetical, but still I was mute.

The doctor went on.

They do, don't they! This was I, Lucia, because I felt my gorge rising.

Hush, scribe, retorted Violet, and so Bertha began again.

He, the famous doctor, told how, on one occasion she, this poor, poor girl of high intellectual gifts, was for several weeks unable to drink in spite of a tormenting thirst. Her powers of speech were reduced, even to the point of her being unable to speak or understand her native language. But I did! I *did* understand and I knew! Finally, she, I, was subject to conditions of absence, confusion, of delirium, and of alteration of her whole personality. And at night, I slept, then walked; slept, then walked. My dreams were purple and full of the nightingale; the linnet: pretty birds who came to me. This, they could not see: walls made by my vibrant imagination keep me free, them out.

*Intermittent somnambulism* went the notes.

Oh but I was ill. Inside, though, Dr Freud, Dr Breuer, I knew who I was, but I could not speak it. And later, as Bertha, pronounced better, I was sometimes ill again. Your talking cures did not wrest this from me, but still I was strong! I have learned, and I won't have been the only one, that you do not have to be completely well to care, love, or dance. To work. And anyway: define *well*. Then *mad*. I challenge you.

Freud spoke of Dr Breuer; knew and saw that he was kind (so much was true) and saw and knew that I was sharp-witted. And he spoke of my melancholy phantasies; the daydreams sometimes characterized by poetic beauty, and their starting-point was as a rule the position of a girl at her father's sickbed. She was me, looking out of the window at the beautiful counterpane of life and back to the bed, to the sparrow on the window sill, the little nightingale I sometimes heard, so pretty, and out again to the sad man mouthing his story into the day when no-one heard. *There was a boy...* thought I. He was a kind man, Breuer, of course, and I could joke with him. I talked and talked and talked; polyglot, running through all my languages, some more natural than others at times, and we christened this novel kind of treatment *the talking cure*. I mentioned it before. It's mine, you know! A catching sort of title, you might say. I also called our discussions *chimney sweeping* and made Dr Breuer laugh and I'm sure Dr Freud found it novel. I liked the idea of renewing: out goes the dust and soot and up burns a clear bright flame. I saw it. I heard the rush of fire up the chastened chimney on the lower floors of my house and I felt cleaner and brighter and I swept my mind clean.

Under his hypnosis I could remember terrible things that were too filthy, perhaps. My hair strung around my face like cruel black snakes; a dog snuffling up a glass of water on a hot day, the drool around its mouth slapping back against the table and the cool elm boards: disgust. I was frightened of snakes and water I would not drink. Dr Breuer helped me to remember, but the work I did myself, through fear and fire. He gave me a glass of water in that long, hot summer and it repulsed me: my imagination was strong and I saw the ragged muzzle of the dog, saliva trailing in my cool drink. Disgust; horror? Does that not make sense to you? But I pushed through: my body relaxing under care from him, the glass pulsing on my lips, but instead I drank deeply from a luscious melon, told off the dog and the maidservant who let him stray where he should not and I took up more fruit and drank deeply from a fresh glass.

And oh, the sounds, the tics, the fear of thunder, the water— yes I was less scared and I did as asked and what was healthy, but, as Bertha, time and again, reading my Torah or feeding the birds, all those years, I would scent the fear again: a jag of cloud in a clear sky; a smirk from a man; a little mouse at the wainscot, pretty but errant, and I would feel again, in my heart, the thud and pound and know the black embolus of fear. When I was ill, when I was mad, when I was not. When I cried out *Tormenting, tormenting!* in German or English, French or Italian or when it came out as something different but meant the same; language beating on that raggedy drum. No, no, no.

And Freud said:

Ladies and Gentlemen, if I may be allowed to generalise—which is unavoidable in so condensed an account as this—I should like to formulate what we have learned so far as follows: our hysterical patients suffer from reminiscences. Their symptoms are residues and symbols of particular (traumatic) experiences. And this was in his *Five Lectures on Psychoanalysis* and I wanted to add: Dear Dr Freud, you know I am not convinced and perhaps you should have given *four* instead? but this I kept to myself.

Yes, says Violet, sotto voce. What a windbag!

And I, Lucia, add that, though all this theory was articulated by men, didn't Bertha think of and name a good bit of it? I remember that Violet laughed at this: You're learning, Lucy Light. Be mad as hell for that, now won't you! She drew a croaky old breath, then.

So to return to Bertha's account:

*Recovery,* Dr Breuer had written in his notes.

It was interesting. I didn't feel better, but he had other ideas:

Your stories, these phantasies that you tell, always involving sitting by the bedside of a sick person, like those of Hans Christian Andersen, said Dr Breuer.

But of course. I loved tales. I loved my father with a will of fire and all ice. Love like crystal. Beyond simile. I loved poetry, so you see, and had an abundance of languages and ideas beyond the sewing box and a cross-stitch world. I loved a bird too, and so I said—and I am sure he wrote it in his notes, so I thought, *Right I'll give these men a story now*—All at once... close to the window, there was a burst of lovely song; it was the living nightingale, perched on a branch outside. It had heard of the emperor's need, and had come to bring comfort and hope to him. As it sang, the faces round became fainter and fainter, and the blood coursed with fresh vigour in the emperor's veins and through his feeble limbs. Even Death himself listened to the song and said *Go on, little nightingale.* And Death gave back each of these treasures for a song, and the nightingale went on singing. It sang about the quiet churchyard, when the roses bloom, where the elder flower scents the air, or a peony shines—and where the fresh grass is ever moistened anew by the tears of the mourner. This song brought to Death a longing for his own garden, and, like a cold grey mist, he passed out of the window. And I am sure you know this story; it seems to me a beautiful story whose magic would have spread. A story of bird on wing, and captivation and a new day for the emperor with his passerine friend and helper!

And I bid Dr Breuer *Good Morning*, too, and then I thought, *I'll give you a story, Chara, doctor, you manyak*—strike me down: these are Hebrew profanities—and out it came, in proper German!

*Auf einmal... in der Nähe des Fensters...*

And... *C'était le rossignol vivant...*

Oh, I had tried to be a good woman, but sometimes I recanted my desire.

You should have seen Breuer's face. These languages spilling out. And what on earth did he, Josef, say to Sigmund when they talked about me?

Italian. I wonder if The Nightingale is best in its glories, don't *you*, Doctor? So, listen!

*... Aveva sentito parlare della...*

Blah blah blah...

And then, for its beauty and because I learned and thought and learned and thought, so young, I drew out some Latin, from my treasure house of things forbidden. My parents had rather I'd been born a boy. That was not hidden from me and, when I was sixteen, I left school and was instead compelled to learn to prepare kosher food, understand home economy and spend days full of needlework. I raged. My younger brother Wilhelm, meanwhile, was attending high school, doing well. He would whine and complain about the boredom and confinement of his lessons and, once, not being the good little lady I was made to be, I picked up my needlework basket and hurled it at him, shrieking, *What do you know? How dare you! You who are free!* and all rounded on me. I smart about it now, but bear a pride that I was determined to learn and keep on learning in secret. I coveted knowledge and was ever more a votary from that day. So now, with my Latin and remembered anger, confinements bubbling up, I said: But doctor, doctor, what of *erat vivus, philomela, requieverunt in ramis extra*? Oh, aren't *I* the storyteller? Aren't *I* controlling the narrative now, *Herr Experte*? (And I was thinking too of Mother and Father and Wilhelm.)

He, Dr Breuer, was thinking, *mad.* Obviously. *Doesn't know which language she's speaking in; can't keep it straight. These hysterics can't hold it in*!

And Violet spoke Bertha's story and, of course, it was extraordinary. You probably cannot believe all these languages, down pat, for a barmy old bird in a loony bin. Well, Breuer was nodding his head at Bertha, I bet, and aren't you nodding your head at us? I ask you: what do you believe? Don't you believe that a clever, resourceful lady (yes, alright, would-be assassin, said to be mad) could remember all this and mouth it for Bertha? Lady Violet Gibson has been here for thirty years and often shut off, by her own decision, from the inmates here. What did you think was going on in her head? She was thirsty, desperately so. Lonely. Ditto. She had all the books and papers she would like and she had time. That she did have. Decades of it. Remember, she's had thirty years to think about and find voice and imagine. It looks like delusion. It looks like miracle. Actually, most of all, it's bloody persistence and because she has a good heart.

All this I say and Violet tells me I was kind to understand and to take notice. I invite her to go on. I want to know Bertha so much more. I want to know about her beliefs, her faith, too. And Violet commands: Ah, well listen and make sure your noting is excellent. Bertha asks us to look down at her hand, on her lap there, saying: And in my hand I held my Torah and a letter. I kept my handkerchief over my hand, for these are my records of this time and of no man's. Torah open on the Psalms; yesterday on Exodus.

Know this:

God provided for the nomadic Israelites and when the fall of the dew lifted, there, over the surface of the wilderness, lay a fine and flaky substance, as fine as frost upon the ground and this was the bread that the Lord had given them to eat. When I was a child—and I am crying, crying thinking of this now—my father spoke often of this and showed me how, on Shabbat Shirah, which fell about my birthday, we would feed the birds upon the ground in memory of this, and I have loved this time all my life. When I was ill, when I was mad, I missed this time. In talking cures, it little seems to matter what our faith is and that, oh that is wrong. Eschatology; our last things: it is everything, the core of who we are, whether we believe or not. If we examine madness, we must examine faith. Why do these men not grasp this? We must examine our beliefs or our unbelief so that we may come to understand what we are made of. How would a talking cure work, otherwise?

*Dummköpfe.*

Outside, there is the song of sparrows on my windowsill; it is beautiful but it frightens me, too, for have you ever heard of the *Guf?* It is written of in our Talmud and in the texts of the Kabbalah: a mysterious storehouse of souls, a place of my dreams, and sparrows sing as souls are released into our world, but if they should cease then all is over. Our world is over. I am frightened for the moment the sparrows stop singing! In my illness and in my better days, I have to analyse what I believe.

On my worst nights, I, a girl of high intellectual ability, as the doctors described me, I hear them, souls, falter and cease. And then I wake, heavy drenched but sane. And I reach for my Tanakh and steady my hand and I read from the Psalms, thus, that *You make springs gush forth in torrents, that they make*

71

*their way between the hills, giving drink to all the wild beasts;*
*the wild asses slake their thirst.*

And: *The birds of the sky dwell beside them*
*And sing among the foliage.*

And I know that my life must have purpose more than this,
A little bird told me that it would.

And I look at the Aggadah. I read and I read. My eye drops, magic, to the birds and their great stories. Just as Leviathan is the king of fishes, so the Ziz is appointed to rule over the birds. It is said that its ankles rest on the earth, and its head reaches to the very sky. It's so beautiful!

It once happened that travellers on a vessel noticed a bird. The bird stood in the water, which merely covered its feet, and its head knocked against the sky. The onlookers thought the water could not have any depth at that point, and they prepared to take a bath there. A heavenly voice warned them: Alight not here! Once a carpenter's axe slipped from his hand at this spot, and it took it seven years to touch bottom. The bird the travellers saw was none other than the Ziz. Its wings are so huge that unfurled they darken the sun. They protect the earth against the storms of the south; without their aid the earth would not be able to resist the winds blowing thence. Once an egg of the Ziz fell to the ground and broke. The fluid from it flooded sixty cities, and the shock crushed three hundred cedars. Fortunately such accidents do not occur frequently. As a rule the bird lets its eggs slide gently into the nest. This one mishap was because the egg was rotten, and the bird cast it away carelessly. The Ziz has another name, *Renanin*, because it is the celestial singer. And isn't that a lovely word? I dream of its song, always.

And I, Lucia, say to Violet: Oh that is lovely. I want to dream of it too! And she says, though not unkindly, Ah little fool, you *will* dream. I do not know who your celestial singer will be, but you will dream. When we get you out of here.

She's talked about saving me, before. I thought she meant just... I don't know... a sympathetic plan for how I should best conduct myself in St Andrew's. Good behaviour, but mainly things to keep me alive, on the inside. Inside of me, I mean. How to use my imagination; to whom I might talk. Something. She had plans. But now she was speaking of something more practical, of escape and autonomy. I asked, Out of here? and she said to wait. *Hear more of Bertha first and, together, have some adventures.* Violet went on, for Bertha, in Vienna:

A letter came. It was extraordinary. Not by post, as such, but floating, as it appeared, to my window ledge, as if dropped by the nightingale at his twilight, gift and boon for me. Could it be so? Do I see clearly? Time out of time. Hide it away.

The nurse from Dr Breuer's clinic called on me today, now I am at home, though watched. She said there had been a letter, but who would write?

They cannot have looked closely at this impossible thing. Its date, the stamps! Cockerel, emblem of the French Republic, yes? What is this? I rubbed my eyes, laughing. Hysterical! But no, it was there. Paris, 1887 it told me. Five years from now. Then the postmark said *England* and *1956* laughed its date. A pretty queen, cobalt blue, thistles, sceptre, a bird. The letter came from two places, winged twice.

How is this possible? Generations and seas away.

The little singing bird flies far and wide.

Who'll sing a psalm?

I, said the Thrush, as she sat on a bush,

I'll sing a psalm.

Even the sparrow finds a home and the swallow a nest.

I know all this and say it aloud.

Doubt me?

But then again, what do you know what is possible, who has not been mad?

So what do you think of *that*, Lucia?'

Violet was supine and resting. *And what do you think*, I say to you. How extraordinary, all that reading and recitation. Well, Lady Gibson's mind is an ornate building and she's made rooms and rooms and, God love her, twiddly bits: cupolas and back stairs you weren't expecting. It's about survival. I cannot say madness is ever good, but then I don't have a jamboree being sane. Being confined and unable to prove you are not mad hurts in a way it is impossible to voice. I dare not, for I shall scream and then they'll come and it'll likely be the *camisole de force* and, ah, a sedative for my friend and that won't do. I realise I'm saying all this aloud. Too loudly.

Girl, you must speak like a lady, your sounds are too harsh, laughs Violet to me: Round them out, plump up your vowels like I do, like a Lady!

Violet, where did they put that mop, the one you hit Miss Drool with? It's your turn! A lady, ha! I howl.

And she says *I took it back and I killed a man* and we laugh, and the scream of which I spoke is beaten back.

# 6

Violet. White. Albina. Violetta. As I said, I am growing to love you. In doing so, I wake.

St Andrew's Hospital, March or thereabouts, 1956. This, as it went, was two months before Violet's death. She had been very ill, but had rallied and managed, as you learned at the beginning, to go outside and feed the birds. I kept going with her. I loved them, those moments of rushed beauty as the birds came to the little pouches for seed and crumbs which she'd had sewn into her coat, her jacket, her ubiquitous black crêpe dress. She said, and we were in her room: That day, when I had finished whispering to you, Lucia, dear girl, and speaking in cod-Joyce, spoiled-Beckett, I felt... I felt awake. When we had been outside, the birds pecked at my fingers and caught my eyes and *their* eyes were of glass but warm and so I asked them to help me. Cock Robin, little nuthatch and you, humble little sparrow, put something in the wind for me. It is a letter I shall write and it needs to go back, just a little, just a little and to other places. And they cocked their heads and they answered, *I*.

This is my letter. I should say letters, really, because while you, Lucia, and Bertha are polyglots, Blanche speaks only French. Translating it—I had thought my French to be excellent, but there's not much French to speak in this place and some of them, the others have, I swear, gone to pot on Snap and handicrafts so they're monolingual, if that: not you, Lucia, not you—ah, yes, I was trying to say that I was pained at how raggedy it was, but made myself preserve it as such, knowing that you would be sympathetic and so not mind its judders.

And of course, you tidy anything up with the languages, clever girl, and you fill in the gaps, anywhere, if I falter or get scant of breath? Girl, here's the letter I've composed. I've lovely paper, see. I'll read aloud, you take it down Miss Joyce and check it later, will you?'

I said, I am not your secretary or your vassal, Miss Gibson, and she said, Oh, dear girl, watch it with the late Middle English and do observe title, you below stairs! and I thought, *Oh, God love us, when was the last time she and I had any FUN*?

And she read her letter aloud. It was to Blanche and Bertha but also to me and, I think, to herself, too. Do you know, I looked at her handwriting and it was a thing of beauty. Here:

Dear songbirds.

From St Andrew's, Northampton. It is a loony bin and I live here, against my will. I live here with execrable loonies, like old Miss Drool whom I went for with the mop, and I am not proud of that. But I've got one friend and her name is Miss Lucia Anna Joyce, the daughter of the novelist, Mr James Joyce, and she is writing everything down for me. And will, for us.

My name is Violet Albina Gibson, the Honourable. I am the daughter of Edward Gibson and Frances Colles. I am from Dublin, from a fine Anglo-Irish Protestant family (though I went over to Rome—and in more ways than one) and I would like to emphasise that I am a member of the aristocracy, though I cut up rough, because (apparently) I am a lunatic and notwithstanding I tried to shoot Mussolini which does not seem—and clearly this is taken by people here as further evidence for both madness and arrogance—such a foolish thing to do, given what he latterly got up to. Though my heart is heavy, I wish we had been able to stop him sooner. Before he was strung up by others. Oh yes: my father was quite famous in his way. Lawyer; politician; Lord Chancellor of Ireland and privy councillor. He had the patronage of Disraeli, Northcote and Churchill; I had hoped that all these connections might get me out of this place, but no. Churchill never wrote back. I am dying to tell you: I gave him lots of ideas of what to do in the war. I did quite well, I thought. Later, I petitioned all these important men: I am well enough to be released, said I. Never a reply.

Now, the crime that, above all, they said (I am not convinced) brought me here.

When I shot that horrid bad bird, Benito Mussolini, Italian dictator.

Why did I shoot him? My friend Lucia and I have discussed this in detail. Now, I had wondered about the pope and about others; those who seemed seedy or cruel and in places of power and influence where they should not be. There is a historical tradition of those impelled by faith, as I was, to do some taking off and to kill in the name of the Lord and for a greater glory and for the lives of others; to be a martyr to it. I felt impelled, as if I had been on a religious quest. I wept and prayed; wept and prayed. And my way was clear and logical, too. He was a monster, you know. If I had taken him off or if, you know, the chance came to shoot again... I would not argue it was a terrible thing, even after all these years of punishment and reflection.

Talk of my family will likely mean nothing to any of you (perhaps you, Miss Lucia Joyce). Yes, my father; I've told you a little already. I loved him. My life, though, was to be set out for me. Governess, debutante balls, all marked out in the proper place and my reasonable eminent father writing his speeches in the midst of these baying children. But do you know I was like Florence Nightingale's Cassandra. I was screaming, screaming. That is what Virginia Woolf said—and I do know that not all of you will know all those I name, but give me time and I shall try to make the appropriate introductions. By stealth or society— that before Florence Nightingale set off for the Crimea and had angrily scratched down this book, she was not writing, she was screaming. Oh, and Mother. She was there but, as Constance, my sister and guardian once said, 'There were so many Gibson children and Mother was not very strong.' Plus she had to conserve her energies a good deal because that's what Christian Scientists do.

I have done much screaming and been punished for it; now, I am at the stage, in my twilight and more quiet years, where my rebellion takes the form of singing. Florence wrote (solace to me!) that women of her time could find no outlet in 'a cold and oppressive conventional atmosphere' to satisfy their passion and intellect. They were not supposed to have 'any occupation of sufficient importance not to be interrupted' and we were to fritter away our days regarding this, regarding that, doing needlework, reading out loud, and taking drives in the carriage. At night, like Cassandra I screamed because I paid the price for the 'accumulation of nervous energy' that makes such women feel 'as if they were going mad'.

Do you all know this feeling? I am confident that you do and have read all that I can on all of you.

And there were terrible losses; my brother Harry from tuberculosis, and I was crying curses as he rained them down. I am sure I do not need to explain to you about the consumptive brain; of what happens when the brain is bedevilled. You'll have heard about such things, or seen them plain. My darling brother Victor and the closed off mystery. Dead in a chair by a fireside in a hotel and how I did not know. I know, Bertha, Blanche, Lucia, that you have suffered loss. I know.

Loss, bereavement, mystery. Not being loved, or not properly. Being denied redemption.

But I know this is a shambolic letter and I am sorry, I am trying to be composed but I don't have much time. I suspect that they do not send my letters here, from this elegant asylum; when I tried to find accomplices and smuggle them out, I was found out then. Perhaps that was why Churchill never replied? I am not a very good criminal and definitely not a very good shot, but perhaps we can come to that.

Please do not be startled and please read on.

I have tried to be a good person. We had our houses in London and Dublin; I had all the trimmings, did I not? But oh, how I was empty. With my brother, I would go to the slums and stews of London: Southwark and a grimy mewling child thrust into my arms, barking croup. I shall never forget. I gave alms, I tried to help. The sadness never stopped. Mother, dear frail Mother was a Christian Scientist, and I tried and tried but knew it was all gush and tripe. Mother spoke of how illness was an illusion and I knew she had a false God. And the Theosophists were in full throttle. Around our home in Mayfair, respectable people went to séances with Blavatsky and once I heard Madame Blavatsky singing opera and channelling Tibetan masters: the things I saw through a cracked door. But I felt in my blood the pain of Jesus and knew in my body and soul that I must be cleansed and made right.

I was a hermit with Jesuits; I travelled and travelled. Tried to know the saints in the cool of the mountains and the calm of the rock. When it did not work, back to London and love, but loss, more loss, then left again and something was forming in me. It hurt.

I write, but yes, it is like screaming as I travel back to this, though I am trying to sing, Passerines. My friends: Lucia, Blanche and Bertha. I have given you monikers and you are named for the pretty birds who come to me in the garden of our asylum here in England. I've been thinking of you in that way. I think of it when Lucia and I are outside feeding the birds, one of my few pleasures and, our carers say, part of my therapy. Oh, is it now?

Lucia: the song thrush

Blanche: the robin.

Bertha: the nightingale.

What do you think?

Do these names make you feel free?

As I was saying, my life was all mapped out for me. I was to be what the patriarchy decreed. Father's quiet dignified girl. Do not disappoint your mother. I shot myself. I missed. I rallied. A thought formed in the soul. Take him away. That man-monster, Benito. He is the scourge of the people. And whether I could martyr myself for a cause. I wasn't really a very good martyr either! But I stuffed my Lebel revolver in my case, went to Rome, lived with the nuns and did charity, felt my soul fall into a well of sadness as I sat that day in the Coliseum, but I acted. Raised my arm on Campidoglio and got closer than anyone else, whether they mocked me or not.

Him. As if he were modelled on you or on your predecessor, Augustine, at the Salpêtrière, Blanche. The tropes of the hysterics as recorded in Charcot's photographic albums. I have heard about that and would like to say I have seen them. Lounging tongue, hands up, smug-face back, lean forward, crouching beast, grin. All that! You should see some of the poor souls here! He was no original because we thought of it first! Or it thought of us first, I should say. Oh, Il Duce. The rest is silence. For me. More or Less. Prison, asylum, here, St Andrew's. And they thought I was more dangerous than him! I am generally a good girl, but I know I will never leave so I must do what I will do and, in that, I need your help.

I want to tell you: through prayer and through the imagination, the most extraordinary things can be achieved. I do believe that. But do you? Might I convince you?

Lucia, I know; my latter-day friend, my song thrush, she is walls away and I whisper and I whisper to her and when we go outside to feed the lovely birds, on the gravelly patch I call my own, where the passerines come tenderly to my hands, I think she is my co-conspirator, a sort of heiress, but realise that the last makes me sound full of grandiloquence and not conversant with reality. Does that matter, though? Looks like my captors have already made their minds up about that! Looks like they have about Lucia, too, though I am nursing other ideas.

But what of you, Anna O and Bertha, who you really are and oh what things in time you might become? I don't know but sense it of you because I read and read and hear what you said to Dr Breuer and, through him, to Dr Freud. I sense you are clever, imaginative and far more refined than I. Lucia will, I am sure, outlive me; perhaps she will be able to tell your story more, in years to come? Thoughts for that coalesce as I write. I can feel a shiver of excitement. She started a novel once, you know, but that, like letters, records, vestiges of her, has been burnt somewhere. Now, she is scribing like her life depended on it.

And Blanche. Pretty plump little robin. I hear rumours of you. Read of the workings of the Salpêtrière and its eight thousand and have seen, though in tiny form, the painting of you by Monsieur Brouillet; I know some of the company you keep, or rather were compelled to keep. Am I wrong? What if you got to choose, not merely manipulate a choice made for you?

You know, we women. I sense we want to sing aloud of who and what we are. Like the birds —suspend your disbelief—that brought these letters to you, dates and time swimming in the air, just so.

Will you meet me? Be together, a quartet? Dublin. France, London, Switzerland? Rome. We should start off here, at St Andrew's Lunatic Asylum. Here, drear old place that it is. There are some things I want

*to do and some gifts I should like to give to you. As*
*I said, these are my crepuscular years. I have rallied,*
*after so much bed time, because these are things I want*
*to do. And also, I have something I would like for*
*Lucia. If we, together, can urge her on somewhat? They*
*would all be amazed at what mad women could achieve, do*
*you not think?*

*Love, all benison, faith in the Living Christ, if you like,*

*Violet Albina Gibson, the Honourable.*

*PS: have you ever handled a revolver?*

*Thought that might get your attention! Must fly.*

*Meet me. St Andrew's Northampton. Gates.*

*Next Tuesday.*

And now, Lucia, says Violet, make sure you've taken this letter down just so and then scatter it to the four winds, when they allow us out, tomorrow, and the birds of the air will take it. Do you remember the little swallow, sometimes there and sometimes not, in those gorgeous Fra Angelico paintings; the many he did of the Annunciation? Yes. I showed you in my *Lives of the Artists*, just as I showed Dr Griffith. Do you know, when he's not there, he is helping me? I've been so alone.

And, after certain preparations and invocations and prayers over the letter by Violet, I did just as she asked and scattered and the little birds were there too. It is a moment I hold dear forever.

# 7

Wrought iron gates: St Andrew's Hospital. Tuesday. It's I, Miss Lucia Joyce, daughter of... oh, you know what: just me. But with *Finnegans Wake* rattling around my furious head. Oh God bless us and spare her! Ah. Stop. Let me speak in my own language because this is the beginning of a momentous journey.

Now, here's a bit of a map for you reader, as we set out.

We should add again that Blanche can speak only French, therefore what exists in this text is my translation and that when Bertha, Violet or I, Lucia, speak to Blanche, they are, we are, in fact, always speaking in French. But don't worry too much about such detail! Anyway, we are speaking the international language of virago and the important thing is that by miracle and winged helper, the quartet was, as Violet requested, at the gates. Looking back and looking outward, where fields and dark towns heaped up; where life lay. And Violet smiled and began:

Shuffle up girls. Pleased to meet you, Bertha, Blanche. Come on Lucia.

Hello hello, Bonjour, Guten Tag!

Look at this place! Our loony bin! They are so proud of their rich heritage of care. I've read the bloody material. Oh yes, *Our history as a charity begins in 1838 with the opening of a hospital at Northampton offering humane care to the mentally ill.* It could have been worse, but I do not consider a surfeit of bars on windows and wretched clicking knitting needles to be humane. But I am a spoilt aristocratic lunatic, so what would I know?

Look. We have to be quick. Handsome gates. Bend in the road (of course! Around the bend: keeps us out of sight!). As this is my forever home and I can hardly bear to show you the two previous (prison, asylum in Rome, and so on), I need to tell you a few things about this place before we fly. But we need to look back at it, not get closer. At this stage, I cannot chance a dash back through the gates to show you my gravelled patch where the passerines first came to me. If they were to see me, well now it might not end well. I'd love to show the spruce and the yew nearby, my back to the windows as I fed and dandled those lovely little birds, as Lucia will remember. Or my room. It's well-appointed and I have plenty of books; was just showing Dr Griffith—I'd say he was my jailer but then he's also a man of some delicate sensibility I think—my book, Vasari's *Lives of the Artists*, particularly the bit on Fra Angelico. There is a Wilton rug and mahogany panelling in the room. For a while, for the family to save money and because the National Health Service began and they let in plenty of ordinary mad folk, they put me below stairs on a shared ward. Cheaper place. Not enough seclusion for me, either. Now I am dying, I've got my private accommodation back, my well-appointed cell.

Quick girls, look back! This old place. It was designed by Mr George Wallet of the Bethlem Hospital, and funded in large part from the reserves of the by-then-disbanded Northamptonshire Yeomanry. *Yeomanry*? That rings a bell.

I will definitely talk a lot. I've been stopped up, with Lucia feeling the full verbiage of late.

*Just don't do the cod-Joyce, please, I implore you*, say I. *Keep it toned down or you'll lose your audience.*

Violet continues: The original architecture is still appreciated by patients, who enjoy the interiors of our Main Building and the parkland which surrounds it. Oh yes, we do appreciate it so. It is a fine old place, but it is still a place of desolate proportions because its doors are locked and most of its windows are barred, never mind the beautifully appointed Chesterfields and the country house aspect. The 106-acre estate at Northampton includes the chapel of 1863—and may I make it clear that I want a Catholic burial with the correct rites and to be laid in the proper place; not because I am of posh stock, but because I went over to Rome, I mean!—yes, the chapel was designed by Sir Gilbert Scott, famous for The Midland Grand Hotel at St Pancras Station and the Albert Memorial. Ah that hotel. I stayed there once and it was a sight to behold. Grand staircases, gold leaf on the walls, fireplace in every room, hydraulic lifts and revolving doors.

Revolving doors? Ha! The story of my life. Perhaps it contained a panopticon, too, and secretly spied on its guests, some of whom may have been lunatics.

*Violet*, say I, *don't go too fast. You'll upset yourself and it's hard to follow.* Then I think, *Oh God, dear old bird, I want to derail her, but...*

Ahem, Lucia. Yes. Closed its doors in 1935. That hotel, I mean. Keep up. Did I say it had a ladies' smoking room? That was my favourite and I would sneak up there to those lovely women and imbibe a little and Mother didn't notice. Sometimes I snuck to the men's room, just to shock. Oh yes yes yes. I am like a guide to the place, to our hospital, am I not?

Yes, Bethlem. Mr George Wallet of Bethlem designed our asylum. Blanche, Bertha, you are nodding. You'll have heard of Bethlem Asylum, or Bedlam. I need hardly tell you of *that*. A Church of Our Lady that is named Bedlam. And in that place be found many men that be fallen out of their wit. And full honestly they be kept in that place; and some be restored onto their wit and health again. And some be abiding therein forever, for they be fallen so much out of themselves that it is incurable unto man. So said William Gregory, Lord Mayor of London, somewhere around 1450. I may have had a mahogany sideboard, but still that was me. Incurable and *abiding therein forever*. For a while I was even the most dangerous woman in Britain. And he murdering Matteotti! The socialist leader, head caved in by

Mussolini's boys and dumped in a ditch? No? Sending money to the dead man's wife and child, though of course he, Caesar in waiting, was not guilty. *Oh, no, no, no!* Thousands. Ditches. Putting a wife in the asylum, letting her die there and then their son, also in a madhouse, pumped full of opiates and kept in a coma.

Violet, say I: calm down, calm down. I've made her cross, now.

I shall NOT calm. There is so little time and so much voice. So much flight. And WHO has the title here, dear girl?

Oh yes, I was talking about the chapel here. Gilbert Scott, did St Pancras and The Albert Memorial. Not a single songbird on the Frieze of Parnassus on the latter, though such would have improved it. But let me think. A bird? Yes, I knew it was there, somewhere. Memory is like a chest of drawers, gorgeous little drawers, with mother of pearl inlay, each one just waiting.

*There.* That beautiful picture of the bird. I was trying to link a memory of a lovely bird to all these things. It's Prince Albert. Queen Victoria's husband? Yes, Blanche, Bertha? Noting, Lucia? My parents took us to Osborne House on the Isle of Wight and I have always remembered it. Precious memories on that little private beach, eagles aplenty and this: in Queen Victoria's sitting room, a lovely watercolour, framed within an arched mount, of a young woman in Greco-Roman dress, seated in profile to the right with her left foot on a footstool, and her right hand holding a sparrow to her lips; the bird is calm and she I think she whispers to it. There is a rather luscious leopard skin by her feet and beyond them both, a sunlit garden; *A. Bouvier* inscribed lower left. Did you know that Albert, the queen's consort, had this ordered for a Christmas present in 1861? When you were tiny children, Bertha, Blanche. But her beloved died on the fourteenth of December, and there was she, in blacks for years and years, and this lovely picture in the sitting room. As a child, I could not get it out of my head. Was the sparrow a prisoner, set back in its gilded cage, or did it simply love the young woman who whispered to it and caressed it so? What did Victoria think when she regarded it?

Can you two stand to listen on? I, Lucia, ask, though my heart is warm.

Well we read the letter and that was wordy, yes, so we were sort of prepared, replies Bertha.

I shall make you call me Lady Gibson in a moment! I have a lot to get out. Time is of the essence and I've felt restrained for so long. Now, as for the yeomen... You remember. Let me think. Yeomanry—St Andrew's, our lovely asylum paid for with reserves from the then-disbanded Northamptonshire Yeomanry; yeomen, *yeoman*. The word sparks an image too. Let me think. Yes. The Chaucer I read. Our governess in Merrion Square read it with me. It was because I'd got cross about our shabby reading. I shouted at her once: Give me something more challenging. So. *The Canterbury Tales* and the Canon, the alchemist. Yes, 'The Canon Yeoman's Tale'—that was it!

*But al thyng which that shineth as the gold*
*Nis nat gold, as that I have herd it told...*

And isn't that true? A gilded cage is still a cage and the things I should have held dear, the balls, fine gowns, *all all all*, were sham gold, at least to me.

Please bear with me. I know I can be disjointed, or at least seem so. But my imagination is violent and necessary because my freedom was taken away. They closed my case. I knew. I heard them talk. But still they kept me here.

Poor thing, again. She's calmer and the others understood and tried their best to follow. Of course they understood, God love them. I touch Violet's shoulder gently.

I am sorry, she says. I am crying. Please. Hold my hand. Have you seen enough, the sweep of green back beyond the gate? Heard enough? My mad reminiscences of time in London, where we had our house in Grosvenor Square; of the Isle of Wight and a bereaved Queen Victoria, losing Albert at about the age when I shot the monster and lost my freedom.

The little sparrow that the queen saw, in her picture from a dead consort, caressed by a beautiful girl in her drapes? To me, this... this imaginative freewheeling... it is a bit like going for an unsupervised walk. A proper long tramp, untrammelled. in which there is no boundary. A flight for a captive bird. Intoxicating, surely.

But keep holding my hand. It's coming up like a wave now, not being alone. That cry of not being alone. I can hardly stand up.

Shuffle up, girls. Let's go.

*Help her, girls*, say I.

I cannot wait! says Blanche, muffling up; it is chilly.

*Aufregend.* Exciting! mouths Bertha.

But after a few paces, Violet stops. She's supposed to be in her last days (I've heard the nursing staff; Doctor Griffith: I know she has a weak heart.) She turns and I don't think I've ever seen those brown eyes so full of fire.

Her voice is steady: And do we say it is 1926, not 1956? *1926.* Can we, just for a breath or two, feel its gyre widening? In the year I shot the monster? In this minute, as we contemplate. Do you feel the time? Its transposition, a kind shift—tender on us like the velvet wings of the bird; like a caress from the swallow that flew, sometimes, from the pillars in Fra Angelico's *Annunciation.* I dreamed that it came to my hand, pecked nourishment from me, as I had planned.

1926, I say. I, Lucia. I was dancing and I had more of my own life. I was nineteen. We were in Paris then and I remember Mother crying and Father pacing. His life was never quiet and it was the year that Samuel Roth, in America, had pirated Ulysses. Oh, the furore.

Yes well, he, Roth, retorts Violet, he also pirated *Lady Chatterley's Lover*, was an egg chandler and went to prison for distributing pornography, which included, in charges, your father's book BUT we must think of you now, dear girl. Of *you*. You are not dancing now and I should love it if you would. I should be happy if you were consumed by your own concerns, words and rhythms, so be collected.

You're a sharp one, Lady Gibson, says Bertha.

Now. Shh, says this Lady: It was Wednesday the 7th of April when I shot Mussolini. Today, or rather in this minute, this breath, I think it is earlier in the month. This asylum looks just the same; birds fly, as ever, and it is a little cold. In Rome, the weather is balmier, in that time before. Let's not get there yet, because there are other times to see and I want you to be there with me and I want to ask you to help me, to bear witness, but also to make some choices of your own, if you will. I had thought that sometimes we might spectate what we were then and sometimes we might... participate, as we are now.

There is a sigh of *yes*.

I will take your arm, fine lady, says Bertha, straightening her back and looking like she means business but still mouthing a prayer. My *Gebete*, yes? I am publishing them. *Gebete* means prayers in German.

To think you can all be here with me, I say, sparking one up. I've always loved my Lucky Strikes. Oh, whatever would my mother have said? We're where we're not supposed to be!

Says Bertha, clasping Violet's hand, quoting from her *Gebete*, Prayers:

*Strength strength,*
*Send with the flame on my journey*
*So that its light may show me the way.*
*And I will not err from the path*
*Through you, to you.*
*Strength strength,*
*Help me amid the tangle of voices,*

*So that I do not, misled by the noise,*
*Fail to find the words*
*Through you for you.*
*Strength strength*

*Let me in breath and heartbeat*
*Be filled by the rhythm*
*That carried justice and truth*
*From you to you.*

That's one of mine. I do have some hopes it might be useful. *Gebet einer Vorsitzende, vor der Sitzung Gebete.*

I translate quickly: *Prayer of a Chairwoman Before The Meeting.* I mean, I'm setting this down in English, as scribe, but I need to express some things more quickly, to Blanche and to Violet, who cannot speak German.

Says Bertha: Exactly. Today you are Chair, Violet. Strength to all, dance, my Lucia, and let us keep our voices straight and clear amid the tangle. But I do wonder. How might you square your faith in God with killing a man?

Actually dear, I did put that in the letter. It wasn't really that hard, smiles the assassin.

We walk on. We're beyond the gates. They haven't seen us! Where next?

# 8

*By means of the handsome new building, all patients who are recoverable are spared the distressing experience of being brought into contact with chronic cases, thereby lessening the danger of becoming permanently deranged.*

Material circulated at the opening ceremony of the new reception hospital building, St Andrew's, October, 1927

I, Lucia, am writing, still; you are reading, still. I am so glad. Tell me, can you begin to see her, Violet, as she was? She'll be here. Here. With us. Dancing and storytelling. Not there, on the opening day of the new facilities, I've noted above. Violet was not invited: she was one of the chronic cases. And I, well now I don't know that was right. When they opened the impressive new fingers of our mental hospital, they only wheeled out the ones who could chat nicely. Those patients who accepted their insanity and were compliant. So Violet was not there for the public to regard. As I said, I don't know that was right. Besides being fascinating, who else had shot Mussolini and made history? Still, I see they might not want her over tea and cakes, fairly wittering about saints and guns and martyrdom. Bet Miss Drool was there, snaffling up the Jaffa cakes, new that year! Then, I was in Paris, dancing. But it was short lived. Though I've noticed that Jaffa cakes made it through, without cessation.

Enough on me. Here, Violet is welcome, as she has welcomed us. Violet and her friends look back upon a life, into which she has invited them. Violet was born into a finery and a loneliness.

It is an honour to receive this invitation from her. She begins to describe Dublin, 1886:

When I was a child, we were many, at a beautiful house on Merrion Square in Dublin. Father would be out and about doing his politics; writing his speeches as I tried to mill around his knees, shooed off. But he was a devoted father, you know. Modern; kind. So look, there's Mother: she is pretty, isn't she? And near her, my siblings, Harry, Elsie, Edward, Victor, Frances, Vizie—that's me, Violet—and Constance. In the end, in decrepitude or in distress, it was to Constance that my care fell; it was desperately hard on her, I know that. But when I was left here, at the asylum, for all my life, and as I have always understood it—ladies, I do not miss much although I am supposed to—I could have been let out; my case had been let go and yet here I was. Oh, that anger scarified everything. It came down to this. They were kind, family, but you see it makes me tremble when I think of it. It was my fear, you see.

But they did not want me.

No-one wanted me.

Hold her, poor thing, I sob. Oh, I. I don't mean to cry so readily, but the abandonment is so familiar. I suggest one feels it like nausea, or a stab in the viscera. Blanche is nodding her head. To her, the riches of Violet's family home would be some unknown world, but also to her, Violet's pain, and mine, are proverbial, familiar.

Abandonment, says Blanche: Oh yes. *L'abandon*. This I know. All those women in the Salpêtrière, well, we were exhibits. I never had a visitor, but yet I had all of clever and fashionable Paris to look at me. I heard one of the girls, once. She'd been a school teacher, before her fall, and she was talking to another about the Bedlam of which you spoke, Violet. The teacher said that Bedlam was as opulent as Versailles; that tourists would visit it after they had seen the finery of London. They would go to the zoo and to Westminster Abbey. And that once upon a time—only, I think, a hundred years before I was born—

thousands of free people went into the hospital and watched the mad within. Looked at their antics and rages; sometimes, this teacher, said, they would even provoke them, because we are interesting, aren't we? I am part of their world, these looked-at men and women.

So, all Paris came, Charcot said it; brayed it. He was so proud. They came to look and to learn. Did they learn a moral lesson? Did the spectators at Bedlam? I am not sure, but in Paris I could never help thinking that the men looked at my breast riding up, just as Brouillet painted me. They were all there. But no-one really came to see *me*. I was an exhibit and they were not my friends. I was *marchandise*... I think the word is commodity? Goods to be laid down and consumed. Augustine, who escaped, before me. And did I do wrong if I kept myself well, my skin as clear as I could, rubbing it with a little oil from our meals, combing my hair and tidying my blouse into a curlicue line? Should I be... should I be ashamed?

Violet comforts her: That, dear girl, is called pride. Survival. I had no upper teeth; I had lost a breast; they thought me insane! My heart was weak and, for all my years, a tempestuous digestion rumbled away so that I was always in pain. Couldn't even compete in the race for old women at the asylum jamboree! I had no gorgeousness to use, for my survival. But I was whole. Yes, like you, I was whole and my thoughts were my own: that is a thing of beauty. If you think you played into their hands, Blanche, then take *my* hand now. Yes, Miss Blanche, and know that you did not. I have read about you. I told you: I read everything and my requests for books were never denied. You will, I think, always be known and an enigma you will be, keeping them wondering. *Did she pretend? Did she comply*? What of all those many other women photographed for Charcot's catalogues, in spasm and delirium? I think these might be questions mostly asked by men; I am sorry if that is very black and white of me! But even so! My thought is that you were—and here you are—a beauty of power and intelligence and that you survived. I have found out about

95

your past and I heard your song in my heart; I know you were confined, before and within the Salpêtrière; I know how your father punished you and how death never went away, not after the times you saw madness and fits and cried to escape when he wrested you into the coffin in his workshop and you smelled wax and sawdust and the cold, abstracted smell of the deceased body surrounded by arrogant lilies. But now, you are not alone, you are no-one's hysterical showpiece or study—and I promise we'll discuss further company later; imagination has magic in its heart, don't you know? And I promise: we tell your story and Lucia writes it down and it is saved so that you have a name and a life.

Now, when we visit the places of my life, and yours, we have a choice. I shall lead to these places, but do not let me be too dominant, even if, as you say, Bertha, I have taken the role of chairwoman. But the choice of which I speak. I mean, whether to spectate, or to participate. Or a little of both? I suggest we improvise here, but let's first be in Dublin, when I was little. Yes?

Silent assent.

Had we but all the world and time...

Ah now, Merrion Square, Dublin. The Gibson residence.

Bertha suggests: Shall we creep up to the window and peer in?—and this is what she begins to do; what we *all* do.

Oh this room. In it, Mother would defer to the governess and we children did what we should. But I know my young siblings were much better behaved than I. Can you see them, my friends, through that window there? What a snug house; the fire is lit, all arranged just so. The room is rich in antimacassars and we are properly attired. Do you see that little girl, to one side, though? There by the bookshelf. See what she did? Crept along, shifting the tiny pine stool she was sitting on, and reached out to the bookshelves.

There. The bottom shelf where the biggest books are.

See her nimble fingers?

Says Blanche: Is she tearing at the covers and the edges of pages? I think the book she is nibbling at is an atlas! I saw one in Charcot's office. He let me handle it, but I don't know if it was for kindness, because it contained worlds I could never enter.

Yes, my darling girl. I was so full of rage and felt the world was so far away from me. It's not that we could not travel for we had the means, but I thought the whole world circumscribed. I sound spoilt! Not so far from Merrion Square were the slums of Liffey or the North side. Lucia's father wrote of those in *Dubliners*, you know. But we're not speaking of men right now, no disrespect to your daddy, Lucia, dear girl. Now, I am not sure if I was supposed to know of those, those places of squalor, a proper little girl thinking of dirt-floored hovels and myriad bodies to a room. Of murders, arrests. Ironic, then— dear Mother, dear Governess!—that I became England's most dangerous woman for a time.

As I was saying. Outside. Understanding what it was to be poor, or live in a dirty huddle, to be drunk or insane. *Oh no*, we girls were prepared for a circuit of balls and lunches. Presented in our crimson dining room to my parents' esteemed guests and escorted out, having done well. Did they never, for a moment think that this way, for us, our sex, madness lies? Such an ingrate am I! Our house was a cornucopia. Look at it! Look at the upper rooms. To get to them, you'd swish up the broad sweep. We had china from Dresden, beautiful tapestries, Carrara marble. We acquired troves of beautiful things and my father contrived arches so that visitors could regard them properly. Once, I broke a vase and cried for days. I had undone the fabric of the house and it was intolerable. But after that I thought differently. I wanted to tear, and so I am nibbling at those books. Because it didn't matter where we went, always my life felt planned.

Marry well. Preserve your family's Anglo-Protestant respectability.

If you don't marry, then it's your job to stay home and look after your parents.

Read, but not too much because you don't want to get all difficult and not have a man love you. Education up to your teens. Needlework. Always loathed it. What it symbolised. Subjugation. Now, you saw me cough there? I was a sickly sort of child, not able to sport like my sisters, too often in bed with a great weight pressing on my chest. It was a limiting time, true, but it also meant that I could rebel and it not be understood it was I. Like the twilight when all my siblings were purposefully engaged and I crept down from the world of sickbed and vitamin tonics—strangely reminiscent now of St Andrew's, though without palpable locks, limits you could touch and sticky lino—I saw the needlework baskets and I threw them over and rent at their threads and materials with the scissors, then my hands, then teeth. Spent, unseen, crept back up.

And I, Lucia, cannot help it. At the mention of the womanly tasks that enraged Violet, even as a child, and Florence Nightingale as Violet has described, I howl: Ugh, the work of the asylum! The little jolly crafts, the insistence on making a pretty sampler, or drawing sometimes but only in certain colours. Yes, the stitches that drove Florence Nightingale mad! I wanted to scream poetry, but that was not allowed.

Violet goes on (I know they all understand what I caterwauled): Ha. Strange that no-one was blamed and no-one punished for the wreckage of the sewing baskets. It couldn't be me, sickbed; for it to be one of my well-tempered siblings, all lovely around the well-tempered clavier, unthinkable.

Look into this expensively furnished room.

And as you see, I, she, also shuffled the stool and nibbled at the atlas.

Let's get closer to the window. She's me, that frowsty little thing. Not the full shilling! She's *seen* things and her imagination is unconfined. The others, if they see us, will turn away; little Violet will not. Look, Bertha, she's smiling at you. Blanche: dear girls, extend a hand to her. See how she stretches out and she knows that your eyes are aflame; she recognises your intelligence. At this stage, the old crone is pretty, like you. Lucia:

dance for her, just a little. Like you did in *Les Six* dancing troupe before, you know, it all stopped.

I stretch and turn. I am more limber than I thought and, as I pivot and whirl, I think *I will dance more for you... Yes. Here I am. Look at us, little Violet. Don't be afraid. Hold fast. You will find friends, we promise. Keep reading, thinking, find your faith. Best not to tear up the needlework again, but we won't tell. Think rebellion if you can't do rebellion. Thinking is its own freedom. You are not, are not ever, a monster. You are a beautiful and spirited little girl and we will tell this story for you. Find your own ways to rebel.*

Oh, thank you, thank you! says child Violet, as her mother sweeps in and draws the drapes on this fine room, in which a lonely child sits, with her heart beating faster now.

And Violet the incarcerated old lady draws us in, her friends, and says: Look, look. Come and peek inside the hallway, through this side window, there. My brothers learned to shoot. I, of course, did not. But I watched and learned from them. Look at the hallway, its decorations. Muskets. Pretty guns, those less pretty: blunderbusses; pistols. Again, the invalid child does not go wandering; that is the accepted truth. But when father is speech writing and Violet's governess discharged to a little of her own time, Mother corresponding with Nancy Astor at Cliveden (splendid place!) about the latest jives for Christian Scientists, then the little child creeps about the house. They believe that the sickabed is upstairs, drowsy, under a cold compress and the influence (they thought) of Mrs Winslow's Soothing Syrup—morphine, codeine and cannabis indica—you all know, as mad women, how it is to be sedated; how the opioids fall through your soul and your thought is in a fog and you fight through and try and try to come up for air. Through the screams, stenches of carbolic; that squeak of idiots' feet on urine-stained lino. You try to rattle at the keyed door, the bars, the polite jigsaws of the mad women caged, freely, in the parlours. Well, even now, I might say that this little girl has had a first glimpse of hellish things.

How well you know our lives, then, my dear friend! This, Blanche. And how sorry I feel for this little girl.

Bertha is meditative, then nods and adds: I'd often wondered if the medicine they gave me for all my physical maladies... if it gave rise to the hallucinations I had. I was suffering and confused, it is true. But was I truly mad, or just in crisis, screaming and stuffed full of morphine, to which I had become a slave? It was not a conversation I could have had. Would they, however great their skill, not have said *Regard the hysteric and her delusion!* But all those times I could not speak out, then my will crystallised. *When I get out of this, here, Dr Breuer's polite company, or the sanatoriums with their pretty gardens, I shall do things. Big things.* That is what I thought.

And Bertha, says Violet, oh you did. Part of what we can do for you is to show you how it mattered and to listen to your story as if we were there. But now, imagine the child, I, little Violet. Well now, the child would open both eyes wide and go downstairs to the gun cabinet that was in our hallway. Because she had spat out Mrs Winslow's patent remedy that was supposed to tranquilise her, and down she would go. She learned about guns. Take notes: now, the Lebel revolver was also known as the Modèle 1892, solid frame, cylinder on a separate frame, and swinging to the right for manual reloading. Please remember this. There were no Lebels in this hallway in Dublin, but there *was* a small, curious girl slipping her fingers around many handsome armaments—and, as I said, learning. And when I grew up, well I knew what to purchase. My Lebel is gone now; sequestered in Rome, evidence destroyed, I don't know. But I had another. There. And three more. Take them. You will have use.

Let's go somewhere else now. Would you like to see some *really* crazy things? We might meet the Christian Scientists and the Theosophists. Madame Blavatsky of the latter is one hell of a sight and Mary Baker Eddy of the former banged her head on a New Hampshire pavement, saw the divine light, got the healing power and, along the way, became the richest woman in America. Mother was a great fan of Christian Science. Loved all the self-absorption and making like Mrs Astor at Cliveden. It was big with the aristos, I think, and Nancy was a disciple, you know, leaving Bibles about the place with marked passages; those bits that fitted with the theory and would surely win others over to the rightness of things; those visiting aristocrats with time on their hands. And both she and Mother came to believe that illness was an illusion. I felt that made them more focused on their own ailments, but I would not contradict Mother. Instead, as you saw, I nibbled at books and, in so doing, made little tears at the fabric of our lives.

Oh, I am tired. I think just one of these sages would be enough for today, though.

I am weary too, yet feel so very alive.

And these women were considered sane? This, says Blanche, makes no more sense than my father enclosing me in a coffin to teach me goodness. That taught me only to scream at teak oil and the stink of lilies. These aristocrats! Well, *people*. It is funny to see who they judge to be sane and who they... they *bury*.

I see Violet smile, although it is tear-stained: Well *quite*. But come on. Huddle up and concentrate. We need to get to Grosvenor Square, London. Just in a sweep of the street—and you need not record it, Lucia—I want just to glance the old house in Mayfair, our London residence for years, and then, for fun, let us pop to visit Madame Helena Blavatsky in Holland Park. She was the loony I was telling you about, Lucia! Girls: well-to-do London loved her type of madness! It is years since I've wandered round Kensington. We won't be spectators, this time, looking in on a young Violet. *Let's go in.* I feel like participating directly, because when I was a child, I only caught snatches of what happened through a crack in the door. Come one, come all, my lunatics! I never got to go to a séance, I was too young, but of course I heard all about that and read all

Blavatsky's writings, God help me. I was in search of an open door, a promised land. This was not it, but please let me look for one last time.

I had had little fun for decades, but now I was imagining, like my old friend here, a riot and some proper trouble. I thought of Daddy and *Finnegans Wake* and a line I loved—though I may have it wrong—just walked into my head; there will be a lifetime of this, you know. It said, *Bite my laughters, drink my tears... spill me swooning,* and I added: *Why should we care what our thwarters think?*

Then I said it again, aloud. I pleased them all, especially her: Good girl, says Violet and, this time, she's agreeing with me, not blabbing about Daddy's wordiness.

# 9

Madame Blavatsky's London residence, Holland Park. 1889.

After Dublin, London. The Gibsons, liberated by money and unconstrained by school terms or suchlike, shuttle between Dublin residence and London; Madame Blavatsky, Violet has told me, flits too. Rumours of tosh and nonsense have not cost her all her adherents, so tonight Helena Blavatsky is talking of secrets revealed to her, and well-off people from this part of London attend a séance at her house. We are watching from a discreet distance, before we try to go in and see what lies behind Madame's purple velvet drapes.

And I've asked you before. I know that everything Violet tells me to write down asks you the same question: *who is mad here*?

W.B. Yeats comes down the steps. He's been having a private conversation with Madame Blavatsky. A year or so from now, he'll be asked to resign from the London branch of the Theosophical Society after he gets together a group to raise a flower from its ashes and they tell him he's become a disruptive influence. It's the same year he writes his famous poem, *The Lake Isle of Innisfree*. Bertha has read this; she loves poetry and tries to imbibe it from all sources. She tells me that she loved this poem in particular, with its invocation of a peaceful place where evening is *full of the linnet's wings*. These passerines get everywhere and oh, for an uninhabited island to share with them! As Violet and Bertha whisper about this, about a place that is peaceful and of time to indulge in poetry, Violet, having identified the poet, who politely bids them good evening as he descends, looks at Bertha, who says she feels disappointed: He believed in this lunacy?

Well dear, why should that detract from such a beautiful poem? You know, after this he was all keen on a magical fraternity—The Hermetic Order of the Golden Dawn—and I heard that Bram Stoker was a member. But, dear girl, you should still read *Dracula*. Thought: stay off the poetry of Pound, he who found the monster so endearing and called him *Muss*: I will *not* tolerate a fascist, so I'll be banning his poetry for you, my dear girls. Now let's go in.

I, meanwhile, am compelled to keep my cover, standing behind Blanche, evading Yeats. This could go wrong. He'd mentored the young James Joyce, seen me in my younger days: he should not see me now, in this shift in time and world; this transposition. It would... interfere. But he passes by. One day, long into the future (don't ask me yet how I know this) Yeats's son Michael will stand up at a Joyce conference and directly address Stephen Joyce, my naughty nephew (or is he merely misunderstood? Madness sends ripples of shame and of pain through a family), keeper of the Joyce flame. He, Michael Yeats, will identify himself as the poet's son and ask my nephew Stephen not to destroy further records. In effect, not to further rub me out. But then maybe, if things change for me, so much younger than the others, if Violet is able to help me change, then this will not have to happen. Or could it be that it won't matter, what he does, if I am strong enough, at some future time, to fill in the gaps? When I talk with Violet, I do feel more hopeful.

But back to Blavatsky. In we go.

There are clouds of incense as we enter, and those heavy velvet drapes keep out a pretty twilight. Inside, tall tapers and heavy furniture continue a theme of opulence and darkness; in the hallways are photographs of the host in India, New York, on her secret trips to Tibet. As I said, she gets to flit. Here she is by Lake Mansarovar. She looks terrifying, her face lit up like a torch in a bowl of butter tea. Children scatter.

Now, we women peer through the clouds in the parlour. Blanche is stifling a giggle: She looks like a man. A big face like a butcher!

And Violet says: Can you all see her clearly? She has a group in position around the table and others ready to spectate, sitting in those overstuffed armchairs. It's going to be a fine old séance. Shall we have some fun? There are still chairs enough for us.

So we slip in, faking confidence, as if invited. In the room, Madame Blavatsky is already expounding on ancient mystics and long-deads and saints. All higgledy-piggledy; a melding of barely explained sources into one unintelligible whole which people really respond to, in the way people do. She is an impressive polyglot, but those around her don't yet realise that her rumblings and screechings are not real languages but utterances she is improvising. Listen; she is talking, first, about her theories, all bound up in fat volumes. I know, whispers Violet, that our smiles mock at her moon face, jesting at her big jowls all wrapped up in a massive shawl, but it wasn't all bad, you know. Theosophy was, at least, inclusive. Everyone could do it, everyone was welcome.

Well, Violet, say I, a bit like madness, then. Though not necessarily going back the other way, When you try to convince them you're sane, I mean. You cannot come in then. They see the fervour in your eye and they know you are a feeble.

And I think, as I listen to the Blavatsky drivel, that some of it sounds, in its dreadful confidence, like the odd diagnosis I've had. *Oh Miss Joyce, is it this... Oh Miss Joyce if you will only join the dots... Oh Mr Joyce, if your daughter will only respond to enemas and sitz baths...* Then I think... *qua qua qua...*

Absolutely to the point, Lucia. Excellent. A bit like madness. Violet is brisk: Now attend, dear girl. I need you all just to see this, mainly for entertainment, but also because—I've asked it before and I am sure you have too—who do we say is mad here? Now, as I said, she's talking about her theories.

Madame Blavatsky's words in a breathy torrent thus: Well, ahhhhh, let me explain to you about the astral perispirit! The astral perispirit is contained and confined within the physical body as ether in a bottle, or magnetism...

Blanche calls: Oh spare me from more of that! I never want to hear again about magnets or healing. What *merde*!

Shhhhhhh, barks the moonface. Or the jowls. Or the shawl. Is she a bit like the barnacle, to look at? She goes on:

...as ether in a bottle, or magnetism in magnetized iron. It is a centre and engine of force, fed from the universal supply of force, and moved by the same general laws which pervade all nature and produce all cosmical phenomenal. Its inherent activity causes the incessant physical operations of the animal organism and ultimately results in the destruction of the latter by overuse and its own escape. It is the prisoner, not the voluntary tenantal, of the body.

*Oh God. Cod Plato*—and I cannot help but laugh. *Jumbled up with a load of nonsense and extra suffixes.*

Yes, sounds like *merde* to me! Absurdité! This, Blanche: But at least we're off the magnets. I cannot go back there. Makes me think of Charcot's hands all over me!

Shhh, I will not be derailed-raileded! asserts Madame. What is imagination? Psychologists tell us that it is the plastic or creative power of the soul, but materialists confound it with fancy. The radical difference between the two was, however, so thoroughly indicated by Wordsworth, in the preface to his *Lyrical Ballads*, that it is no longer excusable to interchange the words. Imagination, Pythagoras maintained to be the remembrance of precedent spiritual, mental, and physical states, while fancy is the disorderly production of the material brain.

Ah now, hang on, says Violet: She's got a point there, though probably accidentally. About the imagination. What it can do and as for the *Lyrical Ballads*, well yes, Coleridge and

Wordsworth had a point. If fancy is fritter, then imagination is power.

And who might yooooo be? says the great moon face in our direction.

Oh, adherents, Madame Blavatsky, replies Violet, bowing slightly.

Well sit downal! Now, you were asking, dear (to a richly dressed but sickly-looking lady) about death. I have good news for you there and shall give you a clear answer and, I hope, great comfortal in such clarityal. Annihilation means, with the Buddhistical philosophy, only a dispersion of matter, in whatever form or semblance of form it may be; for everything that bears a shape was created, and thus must sooner or later perish and change that shape; therefore, as something temporary, though seeming to be permanent, it is but an illusion, Maya; for, as eternity has neither beginning nor endage, the more or less prolonged duration of some particular form passes, as it were, like an instantaneous flash of lightning. Before we have the time to realise that we have seen it, it is gone and passed away for ever; hence, even our astral bodies, pure ether, are but illusions of matter, so long as they retain their terrestrial outline. The latter changes, says the Buddhist, according to the merits or demerits of the person during his lifetime, and this is metempsychosis. When the spiritual entity breaks loose for ever from every particle of matter, then only it enters upon the eternal and unchangeable Nirvana. He exists in spirit, in nothing; as a form, a shape, a semblance, he is completely annihilated, and thus will die no more, for spirit alone is no Maya, but the only REALITY in an illusionary universe of ever-passing forms.

Yes. Indeedal-all.

And are there further questions?

I do think that, accidentally, she's onto something about reality, though. I just cannot articulate it yet. Something about it being an illusion, don't you think? But no. There are no questions for Helena Blavatsky. The participants are exhausted. *But Oh Lord,* say I, *What is it with all the pressing definite articles and those bloody suffixes added all over?*

Have you not read your own father's work? This, Violet.

Madame Blavatsky glares at us: We will begin.

The lights go dim.

Just watch them, whispers Violet: These séances are very inclusive. So she has rich and poor appearing, the odd social outcast and tries to mix it all up—a stew of Jewish and Hindu mysticism, garnished with gobbets and dollops of all sorts. Does voices like amateur dramatics, but her audience laps it up. Her séance practices have already all been debunked, from her time in India, I know. She had bedsheets on strings, a strange trap door and mirror contraption was her Magic Materialisation Cabinet. If your eyes are alive to it, you'll see the seams, even in this darkness.

There are rattles and howls: Ohhhh, spirits, speak to us! and Madame Blavatsky gurgles and chants. An old boy speaks, had a barge on the river, a bad boy; there's a dowager from Chelsea. They have a lovely conversation. Someone from the East End, an old Jewish man who reckons he started the craze for fish and chips and on and on. Some people have dead relatives appear, although they are not named, until the relatives present name them and Madame Blavatsky concurs.

Ow! A bunch of flowers, hurled through the air, misses the table and lands on Blanche.

Ah! An empty needlework box catches me on the temple. Both objects snatched up by Blavatsky's hand as she shrieks: Both deemed to be true possessions of the departed, yes? Some of your sister's favourite flowers? Dear, she is with us. You believe that might be your mother's needlework box. Empty? Yes, of course, they keep busy on the other side!

There's a bang and a rustle from above.

That'll be the helpers upstairs, says Violet: It's why the drapes and tapestries extend across the ceiling. The guests don't look up; they're consumed by the spectacle and can't, like us, do so well in darkness. Violet is giggling

Hoi! What about the fish and chips? I think they will catch on, says the old man from the East End. We are all laughing so much that, in the darkness, Madame Blavatsky now attempts to expunge us: I already had occasion to tell off Mr Yeats and will brook no further nonsense. Now! Please leave!

There's a fine line between laughter and crying, of course and soon they are commingled—and with disbelieving talk of who gets to be out and about and who might be considered a crazy. There are people in our loony bin conducting more civilised lives, and with thought far less opaque or disordered than this lot. Violet knows this; it's partly why we're here. For us, but also for you, reader: this is her testament and a lesson if you've not caught on. *Who is mad here?*

Violet clutches my hand: But will you walk with me, or rather fly, and hold my hand, as I hold yours? I need you to see another place. I was always so alone, you see.

Poor Violet. But as we descend the steps, friends, Violet, Lucia, Bertha and Blanche, we grasp each other's hands and in this still moment we stop and we laugh. It is deep booming, uncontrollable laughter. We are *hysterical*. We are liberating our laugh! You see, in an asylum your life is supposed to be improved with good behaviour; I'd add that your emotions are often forced to smoulder low or that you might stifle them altogether. That's to escape notice or chance parole. And if you laugh too loudly or for too long, there's a risk, I've found, that someone will think your compass is spinning. Violet got lines when she made a joke, as I told you earlier. As we laugh now I think of Daddy. I remember he spoke about liberating sounds—and this is what he did in *Finnegans Wake*—from their servile contemptible role. I thought it was so exciting it made me quake. Oh God, but I miss him. And when I laugh now, I think of how, one day, like him, I shall take pleasure in grafting and grinding words, in experiment and in laughing safely so loudly it hurts. And what is more, you can spill me stark and spell me swooning! (Or something like that.) I just don't care what my thwarters think! Ha ha ha. I am coming Violet.

# 10

Rookeries. Southwark and Kennington, London, 1902. This is where she has placed us now:

This, says Violet, is more of my London. As a child and teenager I would creep around London's Theosophists and Christian Scientists. As I got older, I thought I might have found a way in through these things. I thought... I might find an open door, acceptance, company, faith unstinting, but even when I went over to Rome, I was not at peace. For me, faith has never been like that. The most remarkable thing about it, dears, was not the quality of its faith but of its doubt. Yes, this was what Mr T.S. Eliot said about that Tennyson poem, 'In Memoriam' I recall; yes, I read this just the other year: a comment I felt fitted me. And you see, I never gave up and through my faith, or doubt, I tried to do good. Certainly, that day in Rome, 1926, but also before that in alms I gave and things I tried to understand; suffering that was otherwise hidden from people like me, from the landed and titled; from the aristocracy.

We'd been talking, back at the madhouse, about her times in London. Willie, one of Violet's brothers, the family's first Catholic convert and disinherited for it, had begun social work in the most impoverished districts of the city. He'd have been known as *A Squire of the Slums*. Oxbridge and a toff with an eye for this place. It was not uncommon.

Violet begins:

My brother Willie was well known in these parts. These are the slums at Southwark. Do you see them, there? Those poor haggards. Bear to?

Well yes, Madame Title. This is what my world looked like, too, before I was at the Salpêtrière. You forget.

Violet understands that she does; touches Blanche's hand and continues. Violet is not, as she will tell you, a modest woman, but now she reflects that she has failed to compute Blanche's life in poverty and that the Salpêtrière was not, like St Andrew's, for paying guests. She touches Blanche's hand again and goes on.

These places are carved up into ever smaller boxes, filled with families whose every day is appalling struggle. In here, or in Kennington (which I remember as yesterday), are workhouses, hospitals, lunatic asylums. A million people live here; such like these gap-toothed mothers in stews and hollows. These are the rookeries that Dickens described. Here your heart will break at the pretty child; the blue-eyed consumptive baby. Filth is everywhere.

I have, I think, the sort of memory to recall in exquisite detail tomes and long poems. I read, at Willie's suggestion, *In Darkest England and the Way Out* by William Booth. I tried to understand. Back home in Dublin, as I told you, we were kept properly away from knowing what occurred in the slums of Liffey, not so very far from our house, but for my brother, and especially after his conversion, to fully know and to engage was important, although he was commuting from Mayfair and was hardly going to move in here. Still I cannot be snide: I did not have the strength or the goodness to live among them and I might have been mocked for keeping my title; I kept it because I hoped one day it could be useful, for my own survival. In this, I was wrong.

But as I was saying, here is a passage I particularly remember. Booth told: Some seven years ago a great outcry was made concerning the Housing of the Poor. Much was said, and rightly said—it could not be said too strongly—concerning the disease-breeding, manhood-destroying character of many of the tenements in which the poor herd in our large cities. But there is a depth below that of the dweller in the slums. It is that of the dweller in the street, who has not even a lair in the slums which he can call his own. The houseless Out-of-Work is in one respect at least like Him of whom it was said, *Foxes have holes, and birds of the air have nests, but the Son of Man hath not where to lay His head.*

I might be in a loony bin, but I see that I have that. A place to lay my head. And crumpets. Tea. Yet, dear, dear girls, I do not think I had fully understood that even below what we see here, all of us, is another layer. The person who walks all night, who sleeps on the Embankment or underneath the arches. And working all night, gutter all day: the child sold into prostitution by her mother. Here, in these buildings, I went to give alms and I stood back a little because I was ashamed of what I had and ashamed of myself and of my unhappiness. I was ashamed of my abiding grief and of my illness. I did the same on my last visits to Rome, the one where I shot first myself and, later, Mussolini. I portioned out alms and kept them all safe and regimented while I went to the most unsafe quarters of Rome. I thought it was part of my calling; part of a mission—to martyrdom, like the early Christians in Rome who cared for the sick and the poor. But I was not strong enough.

What we are looking at now is Tabard Street in Southwark. I read that it was demolished in 1916. Do you know that in these places, heaps of bodies to a room, sometimes the landlord removed the door if tenants were a little late with rent? We should not, cannot go inside. It would be wrong and we are in the way. These people are desperate victims and prisons come in many shapes and sizes. At St George's Fields, just streets away, is Bedlam. Such a famous lunatic asylum! This, too, had been a place of little sanitation; where the incontinent were kept in straw and where, Willie once told me, many had been chained and naked, where there was little diagnosis and where a harness kept some in place for decades. You already described, sweet Blanche, what you overheard at the Salpêtrière. This, still, is the history of people like us and one of my dying wishes is that it should never be. Never be again. Had I been well and strong, understood to be recovered, or at least to be allowed to do productive things, I could have done so much more. Because I had a notion of madness and knew the effects of being shut up and away. Oh…

Let me say, Violet (and Bertha places a kind hand on her friend's arm) that places beyond hope I had seen when I began my work and to build the home at Neu-Isenburg, for abandoned young women, their babies and children. *I understand*. And I knew madness and fear. As for Bedlam? I had heard of that and know it to be an old place, shifting its site for centuries, its words creeping into the English language, even.

And I know of locks and bare boards and filth. Of restraints and a tiny patch of blue sky, adds Blanche. Yes, even though I had performance privileges above others, I was still housed in a cell.

Then I: Oh Violet. The *camisole de force*: bundled into the straitjacket at my own brother's behest. In solitary confinement in France. In my white jacket when I railed. I shiver at the memory. Violet, do not be ashamed. Prisons are plural and various; I mean they come in many forms and your suffering is not disallowed because you had privilege.

Violet's tears now like summer tempests.

*It is enough, Violet.* We need to go somewhere else, I think, if you will allow it.

And I cradle my friend. Violet is a fragile old woman and though her spirits in this journey with the others appear vigorous, she could break, couldn't she? There is little time, I fear. Where next, my friend?

Open air, she says.

We clutch hands. I remember that I was laughing about how we crazies looked like Macbeth's witches. I cried aloud, remembering the play: Hecate the ward nurse will be along to chastise the saucy beldams!

Followed by King James I brandishing his copy of *Daemonologie*, no doubt! cries Violet, so cheered by love. *Was*

*King George III the only mad*? Violet tells me that I should look up the stories of the monster of Glamis Castle; the rumours of a royal boy locked up for madness and deformity; of the cousins of our recent queen, hidden from sight, tagged and plonked in paupers' graves. Bad, bad Queenie and her mother. Lucia, says she: Learn all you can and do not forget. And I tell her that I will try. Families can be so cruel, through shame.

Now, though. What adventure!

Violet whispers where it will be next. France. 1887. Where we alight, we would be only one hundred and twenty miles away from the stinking slums and the lady coming out now, mewling and scrawny babe in arms. From the darkness that rests, dilating and dilating since the sun went down last night and so, into the broad rays of sunlight and the purer air. And yet, even here sadness is oppressive. But we can change that. Do you feel the tang of the sea air, girls? says she, and I respond, Violet, we do and I believe that you can change things.

She laughs: Fly, beautiful passerines!

And so we do, and it is glorious.

# 11

There are people who, from a lack of experience or out
of apathy, turn mockingly or pityingly away from such
phenomena as from a 'sickness of the people', with a sense
of their own health. These poor people naturally do not have
any sense of how deathly and ghost-like this very 'health' of
theirs sounds, when the glowing life of the Dionysian throng
roars past them.

Nietzsche, from *The Birth of Tragedy*.

France. Summer, 1887. Holidays en masse for the Gibson
cohort. And here, in Normandy, a place Violet knew so well.

Look, says Violet: Boulogne-Sur-Mer. I had travelled with my
parents and siblings. At home, I was hemmed in, like Cassandra,
with my dutiful governess, but I do see that I got to go to places
of such beauty. I am grateful. Venice and The Lakes when I
was ten. Oh, *but*. And here. We aren't far from the estate my
father took for the summer months. I believe it is 1887 and I
am twelve. The girl at the water's edge. It is me. I am working
out a way to get nearer to my father, surrounded as he is by all
my siblings. Mother is somewhat separate. You see, she was not
very strong and she had had many children. Even with all the
help, I wonder if there were not enough space to accommodate
us all, least of all me, the spark-eyed child that tantrummed and
howled. Will you watch with me?

And of course we will. I tell her that on the French coast I
discovered an ease and liberty I had only dreamed of before.

I felt a new and glowing life within me. Seeing the coast now strikes a chord, strikes up a cadence, both painful and glorious. When I danced with my troupe, *Les Six*, my teacher, who was like a mother to me, Margaret Morris, would talk to us about how dance was for everyone. We could not all dance in the same way, but we could all dance. Dance gave you strength and health. It healed the enervated and confused new mother; it helped the child grow strong and lithe. There was an admirable strength in her, Margaret, a potency that you couldn't take your eyes off. She radiated health and hoped the same of us, and would have us dance in the open air and, for joy, in the sea. I thought she was a goddess. Margaret was the granddaughter of William Morris, you know. She believed in beauty but also in usefulness. In purpose.

We would come and stay—no, not on this coast. I am sorry, it feels so long ago—it was at Juan-les-Pins; it is in the Alpes-Maritimes, on the Côte-d'Azur. Margaret took us there for summer school and we lived right on the sea. Yes: the Hôtel Beau Site. Sometimes we walked (or did I dream this?) in the deep forests of the Cap d'Antibes peninsula with their shadowy coolness, all in contrast with the violet grapevines and the luscious gardens where they grew peaches. *I can see it*. And, oh: it is on my palate too! *Delicious*. And in the bathing hut there was lemonade and I remember the rough rasp of towels on my legs, the tug of my bathing suit and the stretches to warm up that made me shine my breastbone up to the sky, feet in the water, and my heart was soaked with joy.

*And I want to feel that now. I want to run and dance on this beach* I tell them. And, as Bertha and Blanche tell me that they have never seen the sea, my pulse quickens.

Then—and I think that Violet is radiant as she exclaims this—oh darling girl, do it. Do it now. Your clothes will look strange and the people on the beach will stare at you, but then you have *always* felt strange, so it should not matter. Go to the water's edge and begin to dance. You've been dormant too long.

*I will, Violet. I will.*

And so Violet's Lucy Light advances. Not here the soft southern light, but the colder one of low skies and an almost-English coast. Dover is not far away, and in Boulogne-Sur-Mer it rains more than it does on the South Coast of England. From Dover, St Andrew's is not such a stretch: a migrating swallow, on its journey to warmer climes, would travel further in a day. In years to come, Violet, in an imbroglio, neurasthenic and dangerous, would be transported from Boulogne to Folkestone; from there she would travel to Victoria, sweep near the family house in Grosvenor Square and be driven on for the two statements of lunacy at Harley Street, before the train from Euston and, finally, before she realises she is captive. She will never see abroad or home again and the walls of the country-manor-like hospital enclose her forever. But then again, the walls of the imagination are flexible. Violet knows what your imagination can do; the other women have grasped it because they had to, for survival, for their creative strains to be intact when they were presumed hysterics, thought insane. Imagination is vast and protean. If you know nothing else from these pages, know that.

But what more of Miss Lucia Joyce, in her younger years? This is my text, so a little story, not at first apposite, emerges. It's just a little story, but one that remains important to me. Once, travelling to Waterloo, the American author Thomas Wolfe met us. Daddy and the barnacle and, I think, Giorgio, too. It was said (I was eavesdropping later on a Joyce conversation) that the tall handsome man—I'd heard some say he was a genius—was charmed by me immediately; thought me pretty, a little American flapper, perhaps. Oh, I saw him, all right: square jawed and dark eyed; heard the mountain voice and was transported, though I did not know to where. Sensed that here was a man who knew about the imagination. I was right! He went out of its country and he went into its country and the two geographies were intertwined. In 1929 he published *Look Homeward Angel* and I began to read it. The second part of its title is *A Story of a Buried Life*. People forget that bit, but it's a trope all too familiar to me. Or to the others. Being buried alive. *A Story of a Buried Life*.

Wolfe was seven years older than me. A coincidence; a might-have-been: a profound understanding of walls. He wrote, of the young Eugene Gant, thought to be himself, that the prison walls of self had closed entirely round him; he was walled completely by the *esymplastic* power of his imagination—he had learned by now to project mechanically, before the world, an acceptable counterfeit of himself which would protect him from intrusion.

*Esemplastic* I murmur now, still audible to the others, as I feel the swell of the water around my ankles, my calves; the water begins to make me feel alive, as if awaking from long sleep. Yes, I did begin to read the book and was struck with this bit. And with the tall handsome man on the bus to Waterloo. I wonder, what if...

What dear? calls Violet: Are you thinking of Thomas Wolfe— oh I know; I read; I see— because he misspelt it, you know: esemplastic. It's from *Biographia Literaria*, and Coleridge jolly well made it up. You know how it is when on opiates. Even so, it is absolutely true for our time that we use the imagination to shape our world. I'm not going all Madame Blavatsky on you! (And yes, I do know she's rambling, the old crack-brain, but I'm a fine one to talk!) You remember what she spouted about this sort of thing? But just out of interest, girls, that fellow Coleridge also coined the word *psychosomatic*. We won't all have heard of that, for I don't think it was quite in the medical argot of your days, Blanche, Bertha. But, oh God, I had a heart attack and they wouldn't believe me and they said that was psychosomatic. Same reason my teeth came out, maybe. People struggle to read the testament of lunatics.

Then let's make sure they listen! laughs Blanche: They've got some of the best stories, too, the crazy women. The life of the asylum is rich in ways they can't imagine!

Keep up, keep up.

There's so much to cover.

Now I, Lucia, walk out just a little further, into the sea. No, no, not to drown but to enjoy. And really, nothing else exists as Lucia walks, alone, into the water, with her imagination properly plastic and not dulled by the sedentary life of the non-compos. Her skirt edge is wet but she doesn't feel it, in this moment. She stretches and elongates her limbs, imagining she is with her friends and co-dancers, imagining that this rhythmic movement is the foundation of a new health.

Margaret Morris, she whom I so loved, taught babies to improvise to music, she saw wriggling toddlers feeling, not copying, as we should teach our smallest to do. Later—later, that is, in my own time—I would, myself, become a Margaret Morris teacher in Paris. Dancing was all; then it was stopped up. But what of now, for I cannot grieve forever? But in *this* moment, the many Gibson siblings play and dig on the beach. They throw a ball, bicker, and calm.

Look at that lady! say the Gibson children, in their cohort, on the sand.

Lady Gibson (Mother) has her head in a book and is sitting, anyway, just a little away from them. They know not to shout in case she gets one of her heads. Christian Science has taught her to parcel out her energies and rest with folded hands whenever she can, though much good it seems to have done her. Lord Gibson is dozing. It's a fine day.

She's dancing!

And I want to exclaim, *I can't help it. I am alive! Oh God, I am alive!*

Actually, I do exclaim it. I yell it out. What a revelation!

I shout: I am, I am, oh God, I am alive! I wallow in its vociferation. Oh!

The children quietly approach me, funny lady bellowing into the ebb. As I sway and dance, as I make shapes as if I were young again, they copy me: they think I am terribly strange, yet interesting. What is your name? asks Harry, one day to be a champion tobogganer and to die of tuberculosis, wretched, cursing, at thirty-five.

Yes, you are so funny! A funny lady! chimes Victor. While still a young man, he will be found, in 1922, in an armchair in a Surrey pub. Death unexplained. The acute pain of this, of loss, would change Violet. As she watches, from further up the beach now, she is happy just to see them run and laugh. Before they are disassembled.

And all the children dance in the water. Young Violet does not come. Her father stirs and she understands that she has him all to herself. He sees the children playing and does not compute that the stranger is with them, with his large brood; and somewhere not far away is she who will shoot the leader of Italy and be put away for shame. I want so badly to tell him that, at her end, and when she is dead, without him, she won't be alone and her story will be told. But he needs this time with little Violet, or rather she with him. And he doesn't see me: there are plenty of people in the shallow water, after all. He does not sense the paradox, the wide expanse of time that separates him from Lucy Light or from the old woman looking across at him, her once beloved. But in front of him now sits small his intransigent, truculent daughter. *Violet.* And she holds one of his hands while he smooths her hair with the other. She doesn't have to keep up the French to try and still him, make him hers while he practises. Her French is better than his because, of course, she's a rapid learner. She has him, just for a little while, all to herself and, even in that desolate and cold place, in the heart of the old woman, the place which more love would have warmed, there is thawing and comfort.

And the child smiles. Looks across. Does she know?

And the children in the surf smile with the funny lady who says: My name? Oh we might meet again, some day. And then you'll know my name. I am Lucia. Lucia what? Lucia Anna Joyce. They'll always remember that, but they won't mention it to their parents because children keep secrets, if they want.

I return to my friends. I am becalmed; happy. I've had a good throaty shout, too.

The children stay in the water a while, then return to their parents and Violet.

That was fun. You missed it, Violet.

Oh, I don't think so, says the sliding, peripheral glance of the child, whose imagination is, indeed, esemplastic, even now. She cherished those stolen moments with her father.

What would you choose now, Bertha? I mean, to do right now? I ask.

This. A story. Telling a story and telling our story. None of us came to be mothers. I don't know how I know that. I am saying it as fact, not as loss. And of course, for me, there were the many children and young people I cared for at Neu-Isenburg in the home we built; the strides I made with them or on their behalf. I held so many babies, of women cast out, or young, so young; sometimes not parented themselves, so how would they know what they should do to mother? So we tried to show them. Sometimes, to soothe, I told stories. Sometimes, from Hans Christian Andersen: *The Nightingale* I loved especially. (And I tell her that Violet and I love it too.) But stories came often from my head. And in time, I wrote them down.

For me, says Bertha, the gift was reading and sharing it. And from that came my writing. Writing my prayers, *Gebete*, and the stories for children I so enjoyed. Look: *The Junk Shop and Other Stories*. I have it with me at all times, not because I see myself as a great writer, but because you never know when a story could be needed.

I was never read to, says Blanche: My family ill or desperate. Oh, and legion. I don't know, still, how much they were able to read. And I can't read much, or write. In this, I am child, but I'm a quick learner. And of course, in the Salpêtrière, telling one another stories was how we managed.

Tell me a story of childhood, Bertha, I say. I feel that I am sobbing now. It is right; just fine to cry in such volume and no-one need be uncomfortable.

Well, says Violet, if she cries too much at her hospital, there is always the risk that things will escalate; that she will be on suicide watch and so she will be escorted at all times. Or confined further in case of unpleasantness. If this happened at St Andrew's, we wouldn't be able to write things down, notes and stories, or to go outside to feed the passerines. Here, crying is unbridled. Because the past—or the future for you, Bertha and Blanche—is a different... *campagne*.

Bertha opens her story book, *The Junk Shop and Other Stories*, and begins:

The door of the junk shop stands open when the bell penetrates the darkness inside, along with rays of the sun...

The story continues at length; our birds sit: time is immaterial because inside this shop are wonders of the imagination and things that come to life when the bell rings and the rays of the sun warm its contents. Dusty old stuffs become playthings or decorations of great beauty, illuminating homes, worlds. That is how it went. That is how it is.

Bertha asks Blanche: What of you now, as we are here? What would you like?

Ah. My pleasure has been in listening to and watching you. In being a happy spectator. Because I was always the spectacle and I'm tired of all that. Show's over now.

And I think, *Yes almost. The show is almost over for Violet, in these days I know will be her last. But for me, is it only just beginning? Would I shame if I made my—our—book and went boldly into the outside world? Could I really do it?*

Why yes, Lucy Light, you could and there would be no shame, only pride, answers Violet. Odd, then, that I'd not spoken aloud.

# 12

Time to see bad bird Benito (as Violet calls him; oh, he's in horrid, rampant contrast to us, her pretty passerines), Geneva and thereabouts, 1902. Violet tells us that she needs us to bear witness to the lakes and mountains where she tried to find peace and health, but most of all to the growth of one murderous man. Near here, where Violet made her summer camp, he's sleeping on a bench to save money; later, in power and speech making, practising his personality cult, he'll make like a hysteric, one of those poor women immortalised in Charcot's photographs at the Salpêtrière. He'll act like Blanche! As Violet has said, she was given the gift of travel and Switzerland was a place she stayed some time, just one of her shifting homes, but nearby slouched a rough beast.

Violet leads us, her friends and begins:

Shuffle up again, girls. You need to be quiet, though. It is 1902, we just swerved by the Southwark slums and the Pas de Calais, but now to a place which became, for a while, my proper address. As much as I had one, apart from Nuthouse, Cliftonville Road, Northampton, of course. I was there, at that address, longer than poor old countryside poet John Clare—and he thought that, when he wasn't himself, he'd been Shakespeare or Byron. I know Lucia says she doesn't mind that at all, but I rather think one should always know who one is. I must say that he wrote some fine poems in Northampton General Lunatic Asylum. They've trimmed up its name now, removed the word 'lunatic' and the pain of Clare has become a claim to fame, but even so...

Violet, Switzerland! Do not drift. This, Blanche.

Oh yes. At this stage, I was living on Lake Geneva. It was Coppet, not such an exciting place, true, but that is not why we are here. You might care, if you had visited me then, to look at the Château de Coppet and that was the home of Madame de Stael, woman of letters, opponent of Napoleon; a spirited lady, as we are. Can you see it? Do I begin to describe it well?

On the soft grass by the lake there, do you see a woman hanging around the neck of her man? It is Tom and Viv: T.S. Eliot, the famous poet, and Vivien, his wife.

*Yes*, I think, *and twenty years from now, my father and this poet will meet, in Paris; my brother Giorgio will be there (I am kept away, away, and there will be an awkward encounter as Daddy unwraps some old brown shoes, a present sent from Ezra Pound).* I heard him talking to the barnacle about the meeting and about Pound's joke on Daddy's lack of sartorial grace. But this can wait for a later day, when I have time to voyage around my brilliant father; now Violet must describe these days, so:

You can see, says Violet, that they are twitchy, Eliot and his wife. People come here for their nerves; expensive sojourns at lakeside resorts. Up in the mountains, there will be all sorts; the rich and famous taking waters and rest cures. Things for their maladies, the ailments that make them too tired to do anything other than lie, hands folded, on a couch. Neurotics, like those in Mother's coteries, or like Lady Astor—but freer than I was. And thus is the terrible, hilarious irony!

You *did* aim to kill a man, Violet. It could hardly go unmarked. I'd say you should not be a hypocrite.

If you are not careful, Bertha, I shall pull rank and make you call me Lady Gibson! Now. I want you to look at someone, not so far away, in a park in Geneva. Shift your gaze.

Do you note the thrust of his chin and those eyes? Under those deep lids, dark green marbles, it's uncanny. Stygian pools, they will be. He is objectionable, even in sleep...

Do you scrutinise him, there? He's sleeping on a bench to save money and while he's incubating his ideas of greatness. He's going to be a whizz with the hand grenades: make his boys hold them for longer, longer than they feel they should because, if they do that before they throw, then the opposition won't have time to throw them back. He's going to tell high stories of that. *My poor little soldiers, shaking, teeth chattering. Not I, oh no no no.* His war diaries will tell how he does not quiver. In the summer of 1916, we will see him leading his reconnaissance unit right up to the Austrian lines and *let me tell you my children*, when war was tremendous, he was not flabbergasted and still ate a hearty meal and mounted a woman wherever he could. One day, his dugout will take a direct hit and he will emerge victorious into the sunlight; he will claw his way out. His clothes are shreds and he's been buried alive but of course. His story is like the passion of Christ and he will come back from the dead, through lime and shit, covered in the war wounds of which he will make useful currency.

Up up up he comes through the bad earth and from the Austrian shell and he will make this into a book for you! He will serialise it for his horrid rag, *Il Popolo*:

I taught my troops!

My tooth-chattering boys.

I will always be there.

And I believe, oh completely.

In *what*, you nasty boy? Do fascists believe in anything or do you lot posture and believe in *that*, in your series of gestures, unbroken and rehearsed?' (And I think, *well some fascists believe in jokes about old brown shoes...*) You'd do well with your stagecraft at the Salpêtrière. Until they killed you. Or *it* killed you because you didn't have imagination to stay alive and unconfined. It's not true (who said this? Who *said* this?) that every woman loves a fascist or a boot in a face from a brute like you. Oh no. And you didn't even think of the name, *Fascist*: just appropriated it. *Does history know that*?

Somewhere out there, very soon, the child Clara Petacci, the future mistress, praises him and consecrates him, little knowing that she, too, will be mounted before too long and that she will be strung up on the scaffold at the Esso station, next to her, you, lover with your dropping head and the bulging eye, stamped on by the baying crowd. (*And did some of these feet stamp on me, too, the day on Campidoglio, when my glasses were splintered and my hands swelled out to there?*) And her head will have rested on his breast as they are shot by the lake. She followed him to the point of sacrifice, didn't she? And that bastard always bragged he'd die in bed! Shot by a beautiful lady, not a crone, or killed by passion and sensual virility. Instead, at the Villa on Lake Como she, Clara, stumbled on the wet afternoon grass, spring day, high heeled shoes and eating truffles in bed all morning while he read his language books and... and... *ended*. And on one day, after a circuit of frightenings, Ida Dalser, his first wife and his son, Benito, by her, will be left to rot. When she contests against him, says she was his first wife, he will have her carted off and she will die, certified as a mad woman, in a lunatic asylum in Venice; their son, his loss breaking her heart, farmed out to Father's cronies and Fascist party friends and then, himself, incarcerated; in the end, kept asleep until he could not wake up. They drenched that boy in opiates.

He did that? To his own wife. To silence her. To his own boy? *Höllenhund.*

Oh yes, he did, Bertha. And what of Mussolini's Jewish mistress, Margherita Sarfatti? So glamorous, so elegant. It is said that under her tutelage and in aping Gabriele d'Annunzio, dandy-poet, soldier-poet, all things as required, and for a while the world's most famous Italian—born to be Duce, a baby man, beautiful, stunted and dangerous—then Benito the elder became prettier, more groomed and learned how to recognise the weight of a suit for summer and winter. But what of her, the fine Jewess? Escaped to Switzerland, rubbed out in the press, never happened though everyone saw it and knew it did: it was not I, it was not I, it was the creature with one red eye... not I. Did no-one see? Another woman immured unjustly; another woman erased.

But worse and so much more. Yes, Bertha: the *höllenhund*. Churchill hailed him as *The Greatest Lawgiver among Men* while he swept off seven and a half thousand Jews into the Nazi camps. I am sorry, Bertha. I see you cry. You did not live to see what would happen, with the camps, with Hitler, but I know from reading of you, dreaming of you, that much you understood. Be strong, for we will come to this and you will not be alone in its telling.

But Mussolini and the fop, the dandy he aped?

The dandy poet fell out of a window while preening and getting off with a girl; never recovered. *She* did, mind. And I bet, elsewhere, Mussolini's whores were laughing at him too.

Elsewhere, a time of terror, while we are held, here. All of this, you will hear of, surely, Lucia; Blanche, it was after your time.

Anna O, oh Bertha, this is so difficult for me to tell with you here. It is of yours. No-one knew who you were for so very long. Bertha Pappenheim, the first social worker, a powerful worker for the rights of Jewish women and caring for children and young mothers. And all this you did while, back and forth, over the years, you fell ill, took time at the sanatorium—you had to: *had* to, sweet lady—needed to rebuild your mind with reading, careful thought and rest. I am not sure I can bring myself to tell you all that happened, when the rough beast came slouching forth; to your work, to your loves, but it may be that it will reveal itself as we twist and turn and try to do and undo some things that should not have come to pass. I will ask Lucia to speak to you in more detail of what passed at Neu-Isenburg, the safe house you made for others. Hold her hand, huddle up, girls. I will say this: you built, they came, they took, and you lost her.

But, Bertha, you are on a postage stamp, aren't you? Your intent and your determination did not fade, I think. They commemorated you on a stamp. As yourself and for your work. So of course you flew across the land. You were saved. Remembered. Commemorated. I suppose all I seek is to know you more, grant you more and have the world see you more fully, Anna O, inside, too. You were—as you Blanche, as you, Lucia—remarkable.

Bertha is too modest to beam. We say nothing. A warmth, though, inside. Then Bertha says: Who is that, there, looking at Mussolini from a distance? Isn't she a handsome woman, dark hair piled up like that, and what a pretty white lace collar on her dress. I can hear her talking to a friend about the beauty salon she has opened in Milan. Yes, she is saying she moved back home after studying all the arts of beauty in Paris. Here for a little holiday before she settles down to her work. I can see her looking at the man on a bench; seems to be admiring him.

This is Ida Dalser, Violet tells her: I cannot resist. You, Lucia, are still lithe and young enough. (I think, *am I*? But it is consoling that she sees me this way for it gives me time… years of freedom.) I look wretched and, of course, my toothless upper gums give me the crone look. Go talk to her, Lucia, dear girl.

And I do. Ida is startled, but will hear me out because—God love me I'm going to try this aloud—Lucia Joyce *is* an arresting presence.

In time, I say (in Italian), you will marry this man, this bad bird you are looking at now and he'll think he's cock of the wark, oh yes. (She won't know what that is, but I took it from Daddy, to keep him here with me.) He'll be a brute, handy with the whores; he already is: can't you see, or do you fancy him so much that you won't? See. And listen to me. In years to come, and not many years, you will marry him and, as he makes his way, he will be your kept man—kept by your potions and nacré brushes and pretty things at your beauty salon—and he will rise like an ugly strutting bird. You will bear his child, his little Benito, and your husband will be unfaithful to you again and again as he snatches your money, then he will marry someone else because he is a dirty bigamist as well as a filthy fascist and then he'll slough you off. Because you are strong, you will contest that you're still his wife and little Benito, told you are dead, will say that the bad bird is his father: both of you will die, in straitjacket or on the needle in lunatic asylums. Ida, before it is too late, keep your voice stilled, find your son. Run. I know a place. It's where I went, over some years, when they let me out of St Andrew's and into another hospital. Llanfairfechan. It is a small enough place, but a kind place. I know it. All this is absurd, a fantasy. But also, not. Don't raise your voice. Not now, not then. I cannot wish your baby unborn, but when you have him, go and do not go back.

And Ida Dalser screams at me: *Vattene tu cagna pazza!* So I say to the others: She's telling me to go away because I am a mad bitch. All my nonsense about how Benito will cart her off in a straitjacket! Take her baby!

We guessed, they say.

Yes, I continue: She tells me I am a lunatic and to get away. Back to the lock-up I've escaped from after I'd *scopato mia carceriera—*

No need to translate that, Lucia! calls Violet

—in order to get out.

We've all had experiences of bad birds. Or rumoured experiences with them, put about by others' trilling voices.

You know, they said I was Charcot's lover, just as they said Augustine was; that's how she got out. Apparently. That's what they said. This, Blanche.

Well why did *she* get out and not you? All, and laughing.

Clearly, I wasn't very good at it, smiles Blanche.

They said that I... I coupled with Dr Breuer, you know. I was his special subject. Bertha winces at the memory of gossip, a narrative formed for her, not by her.

And Lucia and I each had a fiancé: mine died, poor beautiful boy, and I still cannot mouth his name, and Lucia's found by her parents and all gone, so there we are. But I fear we're getting mired in talk of menfolk. Lucia, back on track—Violet is firm now—so what is in your thoughts?

I say that I think I have scared her, Ida; disgusted her, we all have, but that she never forgets, for how could she? This man sleeping on a bench, bad bird Benito, will be her husband. And so, maybe in years to come, she would be safe, though forced, painful as that is, not to speak what is true. I want to say to her: Oh Ida, have this man if you like, Ida. Let him lift your petticoats and rip at your fine lace collar. Be wrested from life by his sex and that vicious thrust of his jaw. Have his child, alone, as he sits writing and plotting, elsewhere, then comes home to his kept life where you allow him to cut you out of your clothes and roughly lay you down...

Then fly.

Ida walks on, but she will not forget.

And Violet calls someone to our attention: Do you see me, though, walking by the lake? A younger Violet. I am reading my Bible and it is the year of my conversion. Father is disgusted; mother will not tangle, as she's still all Christian Scientist. I didn't want to negate anything of my parents' values, for I loved them so. But my soul burned and my brother Willie was vital here: how I saw that his faith burned in him. Do you know that he was the heir to the estate and that, for his perversion, which is what they called his conversion to Rome, Father disinherited him? For me, it was just sadness and disgust and another road I could not walk down with them. I wanted a burning truth. But there I am, that year, and I am fingering my rosary and I think I am in exile, surrounded by lake and opal mountain air. It is not a permanent home, this. Not long after, I will try to make myself the society girl I was meant to be, waspish waist and gown, back in London again. I will make trysts with men, meet my fiancé and then I will crack up. I will lose those I love: Victor, Willie, my friend who never left me in my darkest nights, and my centre will not hold. I will get ill, be nervous, a hysteric. I will stay, for a while, in Holloway Sanatorium and I will know the brass on the palate and the ashes of depression. I will go on retreat to Buckfastleigh to find the true God and to talk to Mary and, in London, I will threaten a poor girl with a knife with my Bible upon the story of Abraham fit to sacrifice Isaac and they will call me dangerous and mad. In my years, I will also shoot myself and miss my heart.

I was at sea, distressed, unable to speak. I think, in years to come, that there will be better descriptions for what we all have been, of what we have suffered through illness, should we call it that. Or madness, if that is our word of choice.

Oh, my friends, look at her, Violet. Call her name. There.

*Violet.* She turns. See? Still fingering her rosary. The years hold much for her and she cannot be what she might have been.

*But she was. She is here with us now.* And I cry gently as I support Violet and she is thankful to us through her tears, saying: I am so glad you understand. But girls. Younger Violet turns her head towards you. Do not call her forward; she is puzzled and will frighten. Just smile at her only, with all the warmth you can, as you did with child Violet on Merrion Square, Dublin. Because you know what it is to be a prisoner and to be sad to the depths of your wanting soul.

Then let us go to Rome.

The corners of Violet's mouth turn up. See? Oh, these fine dark eyes! There is a dancing mischief in them. She is half murderess, half angel. And bad bird Benito sleeps on, on his bench in Geneva, while four magnificent women bite their thumbs at him and he stirs briefly, as if from a bad dream.

# 13

We go to Rome. We will watch him, Mussolini. Be reminded, in having seen his speeches, in having regarded his gestures, of hysterics' nightmares, a rigid body and torrid imagination of the mad and imagined mad. Blanche, in particular, will laugh at this. He is not mad or imagined so: he is a monster. It is Wednesday the 7th of April, 1926. Along the way, something extraordinary has happened: complicity of the most powerful, tender sort has come to completion. Accomplices surround Lady Violet Gibson, the Honourable. I am proud to be part of this story. And I remember that Violet said to me, as we spoke of our revulsion at the bad bird, that *bad men need not be mad men, but good women can be mad, of course.* There's a lot of conflation, I find—don't you?—of badness and madness. In everyday reckonings, in what the papers say. I don't think that's very helpful.

So, Campidoglio, central Rome.

Mussolini has raised his arms. The fascist salute. He'd come earlier that day from Palazzo Tittoni; from his lovely apartment there. There, Violet had told us, dutiful staff would help him along, make things smooth and comfortable for him and he would have admired himself. Hasn't he come a long way from sleeping alone on a park bench? Later, he goes on to his offices at Palazzo Chigi. Listening to petitions, news and updates is tiresome for him. Perhaps he had rather been in front of a mirror, practising his moves, sycophants winking approval.

Violet begins: Ladies adore Mussolini. Young girls; old crones. He appears, next to starched and bleached contemporaries, preening with his shirt off; cap on; chest out. How they stand by, other flabby politicians, not masculine in the way he was. Even Winston Churchill's darling Clemmie is taken in, like her husband, but by different things. Do you know that, just weeks ago, March 1926, in gossiping with the embassy ladies, she spoke of how natural he was, how piercing his eyes were—eyes which you cannot *but* look at. She'll tell of how all the embassy ladies are *dying* of jealousy and Ivy Chamberlain, the British Foreign Secretary's wife, never got orchids from her husband, only from Benito. Oh yes, I heard, says Violet, that Austen Chamberlain was a tulip man. And none of them quite the *man* that Muss (to quote that execrable Ezra Pound) was. Potted pelargoniums for the orangery given by one of the British ministers to his best beloved. I have been staggered by the things which menfolk do not grasp!

And Oh Lord, Clemmie might have whispered over the orchids. And Oh Lord, Mussolini laps it up now. Being loved and spectated.

Though I should like to think, says Blanche, that the eight thousand at the Salpêtrière would have eaten this *monstre* alive!

And after his preening and his meetings, he's here, inside this glorious building. Here is what he does. Violet knew his routine intimately. I have filled in the rest. But isn't she clever? Such a shrewd observer of quotidian facts.

He ascends the steps to the building. He's imagining this place, centre of Rome, across the centuries, as the centre of his Empire: he's a lodestone. He's here; they will come. He's *magnetic*. He goes past the statue of Marcus Aurelius, which we shall revisit in a moment, and rat-a-tat along the shimmering marble corridors of the Palazzo dei Conservatori. Now he has reached the Sala degli Orazi e Curiazi and he halts and he orates. Here is the seventh International Congress of Surgeons and he is heaping praise on them. He's got many war wounds and likes to talk about them, while he thanks them for their work, and, in his cult of personality, he uses his wounds as currency. He's a real man, a hero, an adventurer, he's Caesar, the best sort. Then it's over and he's on his way out. He tells them, laughing (they laugh back) how he's enjoyed living dangerously. He's survived a plane crash, been buried alive and clawed his way out, as Violet had recounted. He likes to keep hand grenades in his office. Bombs. Just in case. A story went the rounds that one had almost gone off, as a cigarette caught the fuse. He pinched it out and carried on with his paperwork.

Apparently, he did not look up and the ladies and his acolytes shivered, *Ohhhh*, but I'd say that his nerve endings had been cauterised; his feelings had been burnt off, already. Ugh. This Violet, recoiling from thoughts of him, proud, rough beast at his desk.

Now, outside the sun is at its zenith and Mussolini strides out; he's going towards the statue of Marcus Aurelius. Mussolini has begun to speak. It is staccato, then glissando, or at least an attempt at such. He's too horrid to effect the grace of a passerine, but the crowd around him laps it up, as his chin juts.

Violet shakes. This is the pivotal point but I must continue. Must press on. But, if we were at the height of a hawk, scrutinising the land below and the people in it, this is what we would see.

Now Mussolini is about a foot away from Violet Gibson. He doesn't see the old crone and, anyway, she's going to miss. They always do. Anyway, he likes to live dangerously. He salutes because the anthem has been struck up. This is what Violet was recounting, when you first met her, with no uncertain disgust.

*Swear faith to Mussolini.*

Click. Then again. A bang, this time. *Ah, a trifle, I am here. Did they think they could kill me*? His face is bleeding. The blood from his nose runs from his hands, which clutch it, the salute dropped on stone. A misfire and a bad shot because bad bird turned his head.

It is nothing! he says.

Is that so?

Where are our birds? You remember that Violet has Lebel revolvers for us all. Remember the detail, also, that while Violet's will later be confiscated and disappear, there will be three more. Pay attention. You know, should you yourself feel inspired to shoot. *She's a sly one,* the barnacle would say of me. Oh, Mother dear, how right you were!

We are in position. Muss thinks he's invincible. He's bleeding and it hurts. But so?

He doesn't look behind him as he struts past Marcus Aurelius. He who once stated: You have power over your mind, not outside events. Realise this and you will find strength.

How apposite for this moment; for the adventures of the passerines. Benito thought he could control his world. He had it the wrong way round.

And while we have a few seconds, and stand near the statue, let me tell you that Marcus Aurelius, commemorated thereby, died of a fever, apparently precipitated by Alpine cheese. He died in his bed and his last word was *æquanimitas*: equanimity. Our Caesar doesn't have time for equanimity (or Alpine cheese, for that matter); he doesn't have time for anything any more, and the singing has stopped. It won't be a good end, but it's a soft bed compared with the deaths he gave in ditches or with a leather cosh. The *manganello* clubs, weighted with lead. The slow bleeding or the decomposed bodies and all at his behest, while he oiled his head and Clemmie admired his masculinity.

Blanche is behind the fetlock of the emperor's horse. Lebel two. Bertha to one side of the steps, near one of the many spies—and she could spot a plain clothes policeman a way off because Bertha never missed a beat in her life—and she keeps him in her sights. And I, Lucia, take the dying Duce from near the boot of his shiny black Lancia. Lebel four.

Or, to put it another way, at the beginning of this moment, his head turns and Violet's bullet streaks across his nose; only a tiny hollow is made in his nose and a piece of flesh scooped out, smaller than the Taggiasca olives he so loves. He collects himself; congratulates himself. But the next sliver of time sees three further shots. Post mortem will show he tried to deflect the bullets, but the carotid artery, the jugular and the heart are hit and he is down, deep purple before his eyes, the mist of his breath leaving him and the stink of the dictator corrosive.

*He's down.*

No time for calling it a trifle, a nothing, now. And with the shots from all angles and the hysteria of the crowd, we have time to run, the assassin and her accomplices. Violet, hand shaking, drops her Lebel and it is later kept by the police; not so the others. Remember that detail.

The birds begin to scatter; they fly. And Caesar is dead.

There is silence, stunned silence. No-one moves before the first wail as burnished wings brush sky, so high and alive above the corpse of Il Duce. The screaming starts and the running hither and thither but everything is changed. As Violet said, *He thought he was Christ, until they strung him up by the heels.* But now, even now, people begin, although they surprise themselves, to turn away. Oh, how everything turns away/leisurely from the disaster... wrote Auden of Icarus falling from the sky. He fell, our confident waxen boy, but now our passerines do not and Violet—on the wing with good friends—recounts some vainglorious things that Mussolini once said: hollow, hollow! She mocks: *We become strong, I feel, when we have no friends upon whom to lean, or to look to for moral guidance* and *the history of saints is mainly the history of insane people.*

Wrong, boy, Violet asserts: Friends are our lifeblood; not to have them eviscerates us. And as for the history of saints, well what did he know? That day I held my hands out to the sky, in St Andrew's Hospital grounds, I thought of St Francis feeding the birds. I even tried to imitate his pose, his gentleness and understanding. And in my retreats, my reading and prayer, the words and deeds of the saints echoed and I was never further from insanity in observing their beauty.

Their words and deeds echo now, for Violet Gibson, in the three sided piazza of Michelangelo's sublime design, with the lingering rasps of cordite. And as the dictator lies dead. So, *a very human, imperfect character who lost his head* in the words of Ezra Pound?

*Always* bad bird, retorts Violet. No woman should love a fascist.

And I say: God love you Lady Gibson.

# 14

*We know that her homicidal instincts though dormant
are not extinct.*

Comment of Violet's sister Constance to the Board of Control,
1941.

*... so you will not need to fear that I will ever shoot anyone
again, as I am old and ill, and occupied in very quiet matter,
mostly prayer.*

Letter from Violet, petitioning to The Princess Elizabeth,
1944, that she be allowed to live in a convent.

*M*etamorphoses. Macrocosm. Let's pause for a moment.
Your criminals are back from Rome and sitting,
collected... where? A field in Northamptonshire, in sight of St
Andrew's Hospital but out of sight of it. So wrote Ovid:
    And now the measure of my song is done:
    The work has reached its end; the book is mine,
    None shall unwrite these words...
    I had always loved that bit of text, you know. And its
resonance was greater, now that we had been to Rome.
Stupendous change must surely have taken place, yet it is too
vast to put down in a single book, and a book which belongs
to Violet, not to *Muss* or an eternal city. Not to a locked ward
or barred window: to freedom and madness, if that is what it
was. But we cannot change this date in history and cause a

metamorphosis, as we must have done, without giving word to the lives that might have been saved; to the freedom that might not have been supplanted.

Let each woman say one thing. This is what Violet asked me to set down. We women are not historians and Blanche, as she has said, is still learning to write and read in tandem with a prodigious resolve and wit. None of these women is a coward, so they try to tangle with difficult questions. I scribe for them, at the gates of St Andrew's, Northampton, where we met.

Violet: So, in Rome, that crowd begins to turn away. The king takes power; there is no pact with Hitler; Mussolini does not take Abyssinia, in which thrust he would have been supported by Britain and France. He had a notion that he would place international Jews in Somalia; he suggested expansion of local shark fisheries. There, said he, monster that he was, would be the great advantage that, to begin with, many Jews would get eaten. Not so, monstrous man.

Bertha: What you told me, Violet, so abreast of current affairs, that he did. I did not live to see the war, but I knew enough of what might come. I met them, was questioned by the Nazis and I knew what beast was born at Lintz. And I know now of my beloved Hannah Karminski. Lucia, you have told me, as Violet requested. She was my dearest, dearest friend, who worked so tirelessly with me. They took her and they razed our work, what we had done, at Neu-Isenberg. And you gave me to know: by the end of this war, 7,500 Jews were taken from Italy and fed into the Nazi death camps of which you tell me. Is it possible... at all possible that this did not happen? I told you, Violet, that we can never save them all, but did we save some? One? Oh please. O pray that is true.

I, Lucia. I say: I remember, Bertha, Anna O as you were, that Dr Breuer asked you to begin your stories, in your talking cure, with *There was a boy* and that once you rebelled and you said, *NO. There was a GIRL*. He might have written down *mania* or that you had not engaged with treatment, but you were so strong and such a fine storyteller and the point vital. But... you know... on one occasion, when Mussolini swept by in his fine car, *There was a boy* and he was fifteen. His name was Anteo Zamboni. Just a boy. An enthusiastic fascist, it was said. Then why did this boy shoot, later in our year, in Bologna, October, 1926? An anarchist, perhaps; but he might also have been called *the boy who was just there*; who did not fire the shot. But the shot came, scorching Mussolini's beautiful silks and hitting his car. Yet Zamboni did not have time to see for he was beaten down, as you were, Violet; with their kicks and strangulation and then a lynching so he was gone. But in his last few seconds, still, Italo Balbo, commander of the Fascist militia, shot with all his bullets.

He was a child. To be with his mother, whatever he had done, if he done it, was all that was humane. They took pictures of him and displayed them. And then, they took his family and they put them in prison.

NO: make it change in our story.

The work is done, the brute is gone, seven months before.

*There was a boy*. Maybe a bad lad sometimes; swayed by currents; up to no good. But he might have liked stories about cats, as my father would have told, or to play at hoops or dominoes and he could have lived and laughed and loved and left. Yes, a different time and an ordinary. And the scorching sorrow of a woman, a mother, never came.

Now it is Blanche: I was thinking. You warned off Ida Dalser on Lake Geneva, but what of the other, the one you told me about, Violet—the young Clara Petacci. Not yet his lover, still. The day after you shot him, Violet, I mean before we were there, your murmuration (you taught me that word and it is my favourite), the girl wrote to her future lover. She was fourteen. Not so now. There was time for her, still, to grow up and see her old man splayed, Campidoglio; not to be strung on the scaffold and displayed, all pith and marrow in her crêpe dress and heels, but a bride of elsewhere.

And Violet: It is too simple, my dear girls, too simple, but not all is done

A plangent *maybe*. A *time will tell*.

History, says Violet, will record all this and may others, better theorists, expound on what has changed; been changed by what we did on Campidoglio. So maybe. You can find all this out, my darling Lucy Light: I am almost out of breath.

One thing that did not change. That Violet Gibson was still, in time, found out, still considered insane, still committed.

Why not this, Violet? Why not this, too? asks Blanche. *Bien-aimée*. Why not?

Because it is my time, my darlings, my beautiful murmuration. I might like a little time first, for other things; for those I miss with all my crooked heart, but most of all, what I want now is what I have. Friendship, a good death, the rites I crave and the everlasting. That is why. And to save Lucia, who belongs still to the future, if I can.

There was a man, a poet, John Clare. I think, Lucia, that you may have seen the picture of him in the parlour at St Andrew's? Then, it was St Andrew's General Lunatic Asylum and he died here, ten years before I was born. Put his words down in an epigraph, dear girl, when you've finished your scribing? Now, as I was saying, I'd mentioned this fellow earlier; been at the old place for twenty-two years, but I beat him at that! Over my dead body will *you*, Lucia. Still, like me he died here. Oh, he would have loved these soft fields where we sit now; would have loved the passerines! Loved you! He was such a poet of nature. Why do I talk of this now? It's his poem, *I Am!* I am going to recite it and, when I do, think of its sentiment, but know I don't now feel alone. And don't see Clare as a poet of madness, with ceaseless beating of breast. Ah, it's a poem about pain, but think how precise it is; how agile. It is excruciating and its story so close to mine. but he's a poet, an expert at this, not a case for pathology or notes in a book. And neither am I. I have fought to keep my mind clear

and my intellect intact. Don't let me be remembered only as
a madwoman, as a *case*.

> I am—yet what I am none cares or knows;
> My friends forsake me like a memory lost:
> I am the self-consumer of my woes—
> They rise and vanish in oblivious host,
> Like shadows in love's frenzied stifled throes
> And yet I am, and live—like vapours tossed...

I try my best to translate it for Blanche and I feel we all grasp
its meaning. And Violet's. It's like a spontaneous song, then.
And we sing *I am* in our different voices. We shout it; yes, we
truly proclaim it to the world beyond and the hospital just at
our backs and we cry: I am.

I am.

I AM!

# 15

No bird soars too high if he soars with his own wings.

William Blake, from *The Marriage of Heaven and Hell.*

Metamorphoses. Microcosm.

The passerines talked before of what, in the wider world, they might hope for. Now Violet encouraged them to speak more. Of what they might wish for, if anything had been changed for them. Not directly with the death of the tyrant, but because they all play a part, in this and in other adventures, the passerines find their wings heal. For now, what would they have, with this new breath? This fresh beating of wings?

These things. Things to ask for, bodied forth by imagination.

So we sit together on the soft grass, in an English spring, and bear witness for each other. Violet asks first. Oh, it was a fine day, this:

Something for Bertha who is and Anna O who was?

And if I had had my way, what might it have been? I do realise I am different from the rest of you. You know, in the back-then world. I got to be out and to do. But you know that I suffered, too. To be so ill and thus, it was hard. To have seen the shapes and turns I did—of the snakes out of the corner of my eye; the repulsion at water; the shrivelling of my body before, in time, I got things back. I sensed, although I could not name it, that my illness was also physical. There was a pain in my head and a corruption of my eye. Memory was scant when it should have been full and I was so afraid. But you have seen my diagnosis. At the country house near Vienna, where I was placed for my safety, Dr Breuer would come and would, he wrote, *remove the entire stock of phantasms that she had amassed since my last visit.* I did wonder: should he not have been more tentative?

But he also said this: Even when the girl was completely healthy, two psychical characteristics predisposed her to hysterical illness. That one, the surplus of psychical liveliness and energy which, unused in her monotonous family life and without any appropriate intellectual work (Tell us about it! shouts Violet) was discharged in the incessant activity of her imagination and also gave rise to, two, her habitual daydreaming (her private theatre), thus laying the foundations for the dissociation of her mental personality.

Yes Bertha, says Violet. A touch over-confident, wasn't he?

Oh indeed. If I ever have a man—and I'm not so keen—I'd want one that was *provisoire*... tentative. Blanche sniggers and pretends to faint as she announces this.

Bertha laughs: Yes, with purpose, but questioning! Now, while he, Breuer, (and I'm sure he, Freud), did think that daydreaming was within normal, he considered me excessive. That in my case the ground was thus prepared for my hysteria; for my madness. Don't I sound like the other madwomen, though? As I say, I had more freedom than any of you, my darlings, my lieblings, when the madness was quiet. *But still.* Bound up and bound over. Described and... anatomised. Incarcerated, but not only in body. Called to needlework or the debutante ball: as proper aristocratic girl, for you Violet, or, for Blanche, to perform on cue. Stopped up: the lauded novelist's mad daughter. Isn't that the same expectation in another context? And I suppose, in a way, my doctor understood this. That I had no... no outlet for my intelligence.

So.

My heart bleeds for vanished women, for us, for you three. I had more. I was out. Looking after the children, the young mothers with babies; keeping them safe and ensuring they knew how to take care of themselves and their infants. I had strong views on my faith but I was also prepared to change and adapt and I lived long, strong and happy in my social work and in boldness trying to help empower Jewish women. As I said, I got out; to be and to do. There were some things I missed. Love. It did not come to me. Children. I loved them. I adored them, read stories—*The Junk Shop*—to them, as I began it for you on the beach in Normandy, and wrote for them. Some of this you have heard, in the second chances I was given, by my friends and the passerines of the air and by their eternal singer and muse, Violet Gibson. But I know that, when I was gone, more happened which, had I seen it, would have ushered in a heart gone to dust. I learned from Lucia and from you, Violet, that they put me on a stamp. Can you believe in such? *Deutsche Bundespost. Bertha Pappenheim. Helfer Der Menschheit.* The Benefactors of Mankind series! 1954. It is extraordinary and I am flattered and embarrassed, too! But there was more.

I was on fire. Things to do and which—and you remember what I told you about my extensive imagination, my theatre, as Dr Breuer had described it!—had to be done. It is as you have said, Violet: that imagination is strongest in those who are confined. This is how I had felt and how I continued to feel.

So, at Neu-Isenburg near Frankfurt Am Main, we founded the home of which you heard me speak. I was determined we would better the lives of vulnerable Jewish girls or those girls or women endangered by prostitution, trafficking or all ugly force in whatever form it might take. I had learned so much and thought so much in my years of social work. And I knew—I knew so well—what it was to be ill, to have your life set out by another, ascribed or described. And I knew detractors would come aplenty. Orthodox Jewish circles thought the founding of the home to be a scandal, and that I was, in effect, tolerating prostitution and immorality and encouraging others to do the same. What was I, then? An owl? A raven? A vulture? No, I was a songbird: a passerine, full throated and determined. As you would be, Violet! So I had to *think, think, think*. And sing, too. Yes! We all say it now! *Imagination is strongest in those who are*—I learned this phrase from you, Violet—*confined*! What could I do? Ah, in order to reintegrate into the Jewish community the single mothers, young prostitutes and their children, who in most cases had been disowned by their families, all these girls and women... Oh, I loved them all, tried to understand them all, well I had to talk. *The talking cure.* So we tried, patiently, to encourage families who had disowned my women, my girls, to mend their relations with them. No, that was not easy. For me, for us, or for these families. And I dressed myself in the greatest cloak of confidence I could and, where we knew who the fathers were of the babies cast out with their mothers, we did our best to persuade these fathers to marry the mothers of their children or to pay them maintenance.

And here is a choice, of what I would have, if I could. I hope, in years to come, so very far beyond me, that women of all walks will provide solely for themselves, should they need to. But that will be the work of another. I hope, too, that these women can be led to understand that you do not need to heal completely to be effective; to be in the world and build things for it. I timidly ask, though: did I walk one step for them, for us, in that direction? Now there is a hope of what might have been and what will be? I have taken a long time to make a request but that is all I want. Hope. Reassurance.

So. All must die. Father long gone, and when Mother was lost, in 1905, I lived alone. Ah, *Mir ward die Liebe nicht*, I wrote in my poems.

Bertha has been so brave, I feel like it punches through the wisp of cloud, warms our bones, and so I repeat her words, translating, *Love did not come to me*. I've felt that too. I want to shout it and translate it back and forth, into further languages. As I like to do. It really got on barnacle's nerves and I'd quite like to go back and do it a whole lot more since Mother abandoned me. Yes, and I'd quite like to shout out, in Daddy's words of Poor Isa in *Finnegans Wake*, *Be good enough to simpersise*! below the Paris window of the nephew, keeper of the flame. He's possibly misunderstood himself but, having rubbed much of me out, I'd be less inclined to listen.

Oh yes. Violet has filled me in on that. *That boy is never getting a Christmas present or gold in his Christmas stocking once I'm out*, I think. Then I realise I've been spouting all this aloud and Violet tells me she has plans to change what happens to my future story and its curation, but also barks that I ought to shut up so that Bertha—who's infinitely more polite than me—can continue. Oh, and I feel the sentiment in Bertha's poem: love did not come to me. I said this already, but it cuts through me.

I think, says Bertha, pointing at me, laughing: that girl—that Lucia Anna—should have been able to do anything. She is so very alive and so full of good words and ideas! And I wish for— oh the friendships and the loves I might have had. And yet, I will describe what follows only elliptically, because love defies description and it is not... is not...

*Binary*? This I, again.

You know, Lucia, I once thought *I* was the polyglot, then the thesaurus, but no! I was saying, I met Hannah Karminski when she took over the leadership of the *Jüdischer Mädchenclub*.

Jewish Girl's Club, I say. (That's enough now, you naughty girl! This Violet, with a sweep of a caress on her laughing, tear-stained face from Blanche.)

Oh, how wonderful she was. I did not have to explain myself to her and she was the only person I told about my past and how I had been. And she understood that, despite my struggles now, my nightmares, phantasms, panics—for oh Dr Breuer, oh Dr Freud, I did not need to be perfected, to be always well to do what I did: do you see?—I could do more partly because of the exigencies of physical health and the arid days in clinic and sanatorium. Hannah understood me and we spent our free time together as much as we possibly could. When Hannah moved for a time to Berlin, in 1925, just a year before your much-reported travels on the continent, Violet, and our travels just then to Campidoglio, we wrote to each other almost daily. Did you know that, in May 1926, I even wrote to her about you?

*Did you hear what happened and what is ongoing?* said I. *A funny old woman in Rome and yet, have they not really looked at him? How could they think she was more dangerous than him, as he spat up his hysterics to the baying crowd?* said I.

And Hannah said, *because he is man and she is woman, because he is glamour and she is dirt, a row of missing teeth and fouled clothes, because he is youth, still, and she is crone, because he is Duce and she, despite the fact she is an aristocrat, is lacking refinement, I'd say.*

It wasn't so long before my health deteriorated and, then, my tumour found at the Israelite Hospital in Munich. But I was not finished. There was work to do, meetings to attend. So. Do you know that, during my last days when my illness was bad I was told to go the State Police Station in Offenbach, the reason being denunciation of Hitler by a Christian employee of the home? A poor girl, a girl who could not think straight or account for herself, made a comment about Adolf Hitler. She did not know! She could have been describing her cross grandfather or the terse old man that delivered vegetables to us. This I said, then refused to appear. Ill health. In my heart, I thought *Nonsense. Cruel. No good will come of this.* I heard he, Hitler, said, 'He alone, who owns the youth, gains the future!' But I looked at those in my care and thought only of how I had worked, always, to set them free and to tip the future from my old hands into theirs, for their love and strength. The hearing for it. The 16th of April... 16th of April. Oh yes, Lucia. The birthday of Charlie Chaplin. How did I know that? Yes, we learned so much about each other, in flight! You did impressions of him, didn't you? Violet told me! Yes April 1936. I was calm, but I was firm. And the month later, I was gone. Right up until the end,

Hannah cared for me. I was buried next to my mother at the Rat Beil Strasse Jewish Cemetery in Frankfurt. The Old Jewish Cemetery. My mother had once shown me the oldest graves there, the very oldest from 1272. It was a beautiful place.

But I was not buried next to Hannah, oh no. This is the story that I have in my hands now, with extra time to learn. From books, from you, my friends.

A dwindling of the work.

1938. The November pogrom.

All this, Violet, I learned from you. From talking to you. Just two years after I had gone. The day after, our work was gone. Did the jackboot brutes have fun as they battered it down, torched, burnt it, shredded and desecrated? Hold me, Violet, Lucia, Blanche. They took many to Theresienstadt, I know that now. And Hannah. Oh, hold me. The 4th of June, 1943. Murdered in Auschwitz-Birkenau. You told me about the camps; helped me to understand. But give her back to me, just for a moment.

Says Violet: Close your eyes, lovely lady. Imagine her there, hold her hand. I want to take you through a way. Could there be a way? Could we have warned them, told them to run? Her, Hannah?

To where? Where could they have gone? Bertha is sure, now. She thinks *Some evils are too wide; cannot disentangle them.* But still. Violet comforts her: Then, we saved some, when we shot Il Duce, but others we abide with through love in our storied minds. She can never *not* be. And you loved her. Saved?

Something for you Blanche? Tell us, I ask. Sweet lady, make Violet feel happy and assure her that, in prompting this story, she has been of purpose. If you had a choice, what would you ask for, for yourself?

Blanche ponders, sighs and begins: And I, said the lark? Well you see, some of it was true. What they said of me. About my madness. I want to talk a little more of this, for who else could I ever, or can I ever talk to, *mes belles confidentes*?

You know, continues Blanche, of course, that a hospital can send you insane? Not to have liberty is prison even if it be gilded, verdant or in a room full of artists and great ones who admire you and might be your lover. So no, I cannot say I was always entirely sane, but I would dispute the causes. And I cannot say, as I told you before, that I was entirely without ruse, because to be such an exhibit meant I was, for a while, away from the others. If you could ever call me a slyboots, then think where the impulse was rooted. When Charcot came, he made things better; he began to take away the cages for the most ill and the pallets with straw on them that served as beds. But who was to say, when his theatre of neurology was over, that these would not return? And even so, it was a vast necropolis, a place of all human decay and of suffering. For the old, the blind, the orphans as well as us mads. My forever place. You told me to forgive any wiles I might have used, Violet. I try.

No, Charcot was not my lover, just as Dr Breuer was not Bertha's when she was Anna O. Bertha told me that she heard people gossiping about that and it does not reflect well on them. Quite: these gossipers should have more sympathy! Yes, Charcot had a glamour. For a time, he might, as I understand it, have been the world's most famous doctor. He could dissect a brain downstairs, a professor of pathology, and from all that gore he could sweep upstairs and still, then direct a room. I suppose, in a way, he was dissecting me, too. Publicly.

I believe he had the eye of the artist and were you to look at the photos he kept there—always he was photographing and ordering—you would note a fine arrangement of bared teeth, happy smiles, heads hunched into chests and the reclining, standing, crouching lady. I was just one. But this is sad, isn't it? I think that he will have given much to history and time to come: an understanding of malady and of our poor nerves when they disassemble and come unstrung or are spotted with plaques. Poetry! But what happened to us, the hysterics, was no organic thing: *it was suffering*. What we felt was pain and this

151

was a dance summoned up in us. After a while, and after he had gone, I was different; I did not quake or fit and no other would have held me in a room, with my shirt fetched up.

History, as women know, does us a disservice. They thought our wombs wandered! At the Salpêtrière, Charcot believed that lesions in our brains came and went; we had inherited these things. Were they stimulated by trauma? When we died, the scars on the brain, the swellings that caused *la grande hystérie*, would fade away as we shrivelled in our old gowns. I heard it said that there was more hysteria in the nineteenth century than at any other time. *Quelle coïncidence!* Eye of the artist, hand of the surgeon, curiosity of the pathologist, digging and slicing.

But this is what I wanted. I have already mused that when the show was over, I would go back to my ward. It was locked of course. Do you know who was there? Old women, scabbed with poverty, beatings by their drunk old men who had dropped them at the door. Old crones whose children had sucked at their breast and then despised them. How do you live with that? I would have loved to mother, to love like that, to birth: but would I have been too frightened, knowing what I knew? Child of your body spitting on your memory or saying you were dead. These were stories the old crones told me and their sorrow rushed at me in my dreams.

There were pockmarked whores. But their essential beauty could not be washed away, though they stank of men's sex and were steeped in dirt and would talk of what they had done and what they had been made to do. I could not help the way the images swooshed together when my eyes were closed. Staff photographed the inmates barking and crawling on fours; reclining; supine; helpless and luxuriant on their beds or a soft chair given to them, that time, by Charcot. The women laughed: Men paid me to do this! Some of them were excited by the filth that we now demonstrate—looked at us, poor desperates, from the mind of a pervert, or a most particular customer!

But I looked at their eyes and their eyes were not laughing.

Beggars in rags: got off the street! Hysterics! Papers stamped and scribbled on, and now the streets are tidier and le tout Paris need not abide its feet on the pavements where the cockroaches lay before. The mad through sex. Through venereal disease, or so they thought. Or just the mad. That was the story of this place. I don't mind saying. Cannot sorrow derange you and the thought that no-one cares or loves and then you are an exhibit? This was an enormous place. It was not a prestigious hospital, so I could say we were lucky to have such a man as Monsieur Charcot studying here; in time, he took away the worst of cages and pallets and chains, as I told you. Whichever of his proclamations must be proved right and whichever wrong, we were subjects and objects: a stable field of study: a circus which did not travel. It was a groaning prison under the sky. Do you know Baudelaire's *Alchimie de la douleur?* Remember the teacher I told you of, my fellow inmate? Well that is how I learned about it. In the first verse, this, *Ce qui dit à l'un: Sépulture! Dit à l'autre: Vie et splendeur*!

It is about how something that speaks to one of tombs and death, speaks to another of splendour, life. I would cling to this beautiful idea. In the midst of what we saw, I must transform my thought, if I could, and find a golden impulse to life. During the rounds of jangling keys. Screeching and the wails for someone to come. Piss and shit everywhere. Cross people with mops and a lovely drawing room, wherein the court painter would come. And he painted me! And I saw the golden impulse to life.

And of course, we notice things, we women. We know where the jangling keys are and where the drugs are, for the most crazy. The hypnotics and all. I know where the needles are because of rooms I have glimpsed on the way to my showroom. We know where the straps and restraints are, and the *camisoles de force.* On portrait day, I was especially alert of who was where and what was where because on that day they were especially genteel to me. *And I saw.*

So this is what I want: Take me back. And this time I don't want to spectate, so you be my guests!

I saw keys. And I saw eight thousand and thirteen women. I am the next digit. What a rabble we would be, if we got out. We are cunning. Shuffle up to the window girls. Do you see her, me? In that room, as Monsieur Brouillet paints. It's the fourth day and the final day. Tonight—it is Friday, nearly their weekend (in the asylum days of the week do not matter)—and the exhibition in the hospital salon only runs on Tuesday and Friday. So during the week, Violet, Bertha, Lucia, you could dance through the streets. Lucia: you know this place, Paris, well and I think you will come back. Violet: you told me that in years to come, after I am gone, extraordinary people will run in these streets in peacock colours and auburn mop-head haircuts; novelists and artists and mad, mad, mad. I wish that I could see it, then. But for now, during this week, Lucia, take these fine birds round the city you know, though before your time—and enjoy it, won't you? Take your coffee and your little cakes and go to the galleries. I have never seen what is in them, but of course I imagine and I hear whispers of the wonders within. Do you think the painting of me will live in a gallery one day? Ça fait tout. Here is what we do on Friday. Our special Friday, when the Queen of the Hysterics performs in the mad salon.

I will have spread whispers through the hospital. *Women! Crones, lunatics, syphilitics, whores: you are all the same for me and we live together. Tonight: we are going out. Believe it. To Boulevard St Germain. And we are going to dance in the streets and drink something good and meet someone you once met.* You help me. Sing at the cracked windows and be full throated.

And the whispers, your songs, will have held good. Our inmates. We stole keys and draughts; things to keep us quiet. Sometimes, we cut up a little rough, but still. We put the staff under lock and, because we are not animals, not feral, we apologised. In some, we saw understanding. In others, not so.

I had performed for Charcot and his good people on Friday and Monsieur Brouillet was almost done with his painting of me and tonight, at the house of Charcot, there was a special party. I had heard them talking over their plans, though they knew that not. I had never learned to read; an illiterate, for who was I, just an insignificant splash of mad. But you see, you listen, when you are locked up; your imagination does gymnastics. This is what Violet has understood. And in her mind, she has spoken with such vibrancy to us.

Words come in and sometimes I do not know from where.

There are clever people in the Salpêtrière and I know, my friends, that there will be as we walk along these streets because I, like the others, have learned to listen and to absorb: sensations, the subtle modulations of stone under my foot. It is not even and I feel it; study. Looks between people and lines that don't sound quite natural in their mouths, I heard one, once. Was it a visitor? I don't quite remember. But when people from outside came to the hospital, we listened in hard and ate up those words, their sounds dripping from our tongues. What do I do? Will I get out? How can I survive here? said poor old Adalene, kennelled next to me, exploring what she could do in her mad mind to keep sane; saying this rubbish to a middle-aged man who came once. He looked well dressed and he said, Ah, he said, The images selected by memory are as arbitrary, as narrow, as elusive as those which the imagination had formed and reality has destroyed. There is no reason why, existing outside ourselves, a real place should conform to the pictures in our memory rather than those in our dreams. A famous writer said this.

He was her husband and he never came again.

She said nothing to his poetry. I heard tears, though not comfort from him. But I thought about the words, though I disliked the mouth that spawned them. How would it be if we could take our dreams, our imagination, our night reveries, and mould such into a real place? Night after night I thought of that. And of course those lines of Baudelaire. Until your letter came, my dear Violet. *Mon petit miracle! Mon passereau en vol*!

And it is Friday. *Fête*!

*Meine Passerine im flug!* beams Bertha. Yes Lucia, my passerine in flight!

And do you know, continues Blanche, now that we are here, in flight, I had another thing pop into my head. Words that were not my own, but which fitted just right. I may have looked ravishing in Brouillet's painting, but look closely and at all of us. We are old. Sullied. We do not have that fresh beauty of the woman on the outside. The thought made me sad, but then those poetry words came as I took full grasp of our power and our cunning. And I laughed just now! *Laissons les jolies femmes aux hommes sans imagination,* I said.

Leave the pretty women for the men without imagination, say I, Lucia. Oh, I'm sorry, You told me not to do that. But you are right, Blanche: it would only be the man of true imagination who could reckon with us! And that was Proust, you know. You are a book, though you never learned to read, you beautiful, beautiful loon! And I love your Baudelaire poem too.

So. Today, Friday, Blanche has exhibited in front of the good and great of Paris. She has swooned, and if you have seen the Brouillet painting then you know how she looked. But this is what came next. Tout Paris could not get out; they were locked in their room. It was not on the ground floor and these were not men brave enough to jump, oh no. There were two nurses in the room, steadying Blanche, before, but they jumped: held her. Helped. They would certainly lose their jobs, but the idea was that, in the confusion, who could tell? When in Rome...

Down the corridors, staff found themselves walled up, confined to their own imaginations while the inmates ran into the streets, or rather while they flew. Some staff drugged in possets, some with needles, in this moment of rebellion and endless time, because what is time to someone who is endlessly mad, one of eight thousand and more, never going home?

And I have taken up the tale, so she can rest and relish it. The rest is going to be delicious.

So now. Violet, Blanche, Bertha and I, Lucia. Now with an extraordinary rabble. The saddest thing: that not all eight thousand came, only those who could still brave the rushing walk. Whose limbs were pliable enough to do it and whose minds were not terrified by the sunlight on their faces and the endless altered world beyond the hospital. It is called being institutionalised. But the free would tell their story to the others, wouldn't they?

So Blanche. In the fresh air. All this time, all these waiting years, she has been listening, having more access to the conversation of Monsieur and his friends than others in the Salpêtrière, just like Augustine, queen before her, and who escaped because of it. She, Blanche, knows where Charcot lives, what he reads and that he plays the piano. She knows he likes to cook, or be cooked for, rather, at his professional discretion and to understand taste and separate flavours as if it were a dissection. She has her energy restored a little and asks to take up the tale and says, proudly, eyes lighting up: Imagine! There is a book he especially likes: *La Physiologie du Goût*—yes, like even taste has a body, an anatomy!—by someone called Brillat-Savarin. Charcot, before he was the great neurologist, was the professor of pathology and still, so I hear, when we die, he dissects. They are downstairs, the dead women. I wonder what he finds inside their heads, but I would bet there are no lesions or scars to see. Can he not see the sorrow swarming around us? Can he not *see*? Still, I heard him talking to the other doctors about this book and, My God, it sounded like a dissection! Of appetite and mood; of taste and wealth. I felt sick.

As I was saying, Brillat-Savarin was not a Parisian, I learned, but from Bresse: I have never been there. Charcot has, of course. I heard him talk about Brillat-Savarin's country, of gratin d'écrivesses, a beautiful Bresse chicken, all sorts of wonderful things; mon Dieu, I could hardly bear the deliciousness. Here, well, you can imagine. Bread and slops; watery cabbage stuff. But I heard him speak of his travels and he said, *cœur à la crème* and talked about *pâté* as an *hors-d'oeuvre*. Can you imagine? I ate up those words. When he made me crawl like a dog, as he made Augustine and many others, we were thinking about what it might be to have thick fresh cream in your mouth. To run that succulent *pâté* across your tongue, your teeth and to tear at a crayfish. And we slavered and drooled and Charcot said, *So you see, so you see! They are suggestible, in this state, the hysterics* and he didn't see at all, poor well-fed bastard. Well, tonight, he has a dinner, after aperitifs around his piano, based on the book with all its analysis and meditations. I heard him speaking of it. A banquet. Let's dine. Let *us* dine, instead. We shall partake of his humorous feast while he's locked in his office back at the asylum.

Oh. Well. Violet and I have had the same menu at St Andrew's. Tapioca. Sago. Soft-boiled potatoes and nursery fish. That's what we mental patients have been imbibing. Nothing to excite us. A little broth for Bertha. Slops for Blanche. God love us, what we want is a feast. A feast. Oh, and a hot and tousled bed in a full night. We're that clever, but it's not all about the cerebral. Or praying. We have appetites and I say to Blanche *Oh for this I cannot wait!*

I am crying relentlessly. Slavering. I look mad.

And so our passerines fly. In fact, we have to run as it is a little way between the hospital district and the home of Charcot. To the east, Cathédrale Notre Dame; off further to the West, Le Jardin du Luxembourg. Nearby, although not yet (I know this, I know this!), is the bookshop Shakespeare and Company, a detail which will be important. It doesn't exist yet. *I* don't exist yet, but here I am and I feel a future for me, at liberty, just to the south-west, as we fly to their dinner.

Magic?

Boulevard de l'Hôpital, Quai Saint-Bernard and Quai de la Tournelle. *Attend.* A delicate left onto Rue des Saints-Pères and so onto Boulevard Saint-Germain and now our passerines are standing on the left bank of the River Seine and the light is purple.

Oh, how fine. Oh Violet, say I and then, *It is the hour to be drunken! To escape being the martyred slaves of time, be ceaselessly drunk. On wine, on poetry, or on virtue, as you wish.* I've always loved Baudelaire.

And much good it did you, dear, Violet snaps back.

I heard Charcot talk about this street—this place where he lived, says Blanche, and he told of how the boulevard replaced numerous small streets... the Rue Saint-Dominique, Rue des Boucheries... There was one particular thing I remembered: that they destroyed the prison of the Abbey of Saint-Germain-des-Prés which stood here. Now, much of the old aristocracy lives on this street—I suppose like you, the Honourable Violet! I overheard Charcot saying that the new upper bourgeoisie have their homes on the right bank. When he said that, I felt he was giving himself airs and graces.

Yes, bloody cheek. This, Violet: Old money is the aristocracy. World famous doctor and he's still new money!

In extremis, she will never drop her title. She slightly disgusts me sometimes, but I think, *God love her.*

Blanche again: But what of that prison I mentioned? Again he, Charcot, said of it that the cells had been so abominable and so humid that the soldiers incarcerated there had to go to the Val-de-Grâce hospital to recover from their imprisonment. And so many of them had only committed little crimes. I think this street will be haunted and, even with its finery, I do not think I would want to live here. And I heard him speak of how, in 1792, during the Revolution, this, where his house sits now, was the site of one of the September massacres. Many of the dead were priests, you know; those who would not swear to the state. When I heard Charcot speak of this, it haunted my dreams; those priests praying and dying and no-one came. I cannot—I—

So Violet counsels her friend: Blanche, dear girl, you must stop. Calm. We have all been prisoners of one sort or another, and as Lucia was telling earlier, prisons are legion and various. In different places. At home. Bertha has said the same. Be comforted. But I am the only criminal here, although I've managed to make you accomplices, so I tell you to let this go, this train of thought. Think only now of the pretty lights up on the Seine and the dinner we will have. I do not tell you to harden your heart to the suffering of others, but to hold them up before God and to please remember that this minute, this encaged golden minute of our flight, may be all we have. Walk on, beautiful lady.

Now, ah: could this be the house? Oh yes, how fine indeed. Think of the other women behind us now. All those pockmarked, exhausted mothers and daughters; those slatterns dancing behind you. They look to you.

*Alors*, I have the key, announces a jubilant Blanche and in we rush, the many, in past the gilded mirrors, the lilies in tall white vases (Bastards! I will always hate lilies! They are coffin flowers! says Blanche) and there is the front room with the piano and its vast table and the serving women, who rush out in horror and then, through curiosity, creep back in, and point to the delicacies and the book, the Brillat-Savarin, is open on this page and thus in dinner. Blanche cannot read, Bertha is exhausted from their journey, and so it falls to me to read aloud, and laugh as I do.

Oh dinner. Oh. Oh My God. Described on the page and set out on a silver bookstand. A recipe or a surgical approach. Some of both! The bastard!

We women have been often used to slops, scared of water and too sad to take care of our own nourishment. Back at St Andrew's food has been sturdy, but necessarily bland, to keep the excitement down. Give a lunatic a crayfish to bite and suck at? Oh no. A slab of boiled fish; tripe and onions with soft-boiled potatoes; broth: dumplings in a congealed stew, and apple crumble cooked to bastardy. The really desperate ones spoon fed. Now, I laugh again, as I read: I read of status and luxury and the response one is aiming to elicit in guests. In a moment, we'll all be hysterical again. This is what it says on the displayed pages, for the amusement of his society; I read it all aloud: Oh la la, look what you get, girls! INCOME 30,000 FRANCS, OR MORE:

A fowl weighing seven pounds, stuffed with truffles, so that it has become a spheroid.

Pâté Périgord in the form of a bastion.

A cask of Chambord richly dressed and decorated.

A pike stuffed with crayfish.

A pheasant dressed à la sainte alliance.

Two dozen ortolans à la Provençal.

At this, we wince and shriek, thinking, *Poor ortolans! They are passerines like us. Bloody men! How dare they!* Onward with the planned excess. For heaven's sake:

A pyramid of sweetmeats, flavoured with rose and vanilla.

Oh girls, I laugh: Just look at this, it is so funny. Wouldn't even a loon die of an embarrassment of riches, or for shame?

Then we all tear at the food, the pyramids and hecatombs, An old woman crunches and chews at the head of the pike, sucking out its juices, while her friend stabs at the crayfish; Violet, missing many teeth, loves the soft rose sweetmeats and Bertha the pheasant. We all share and quarrel at this dinner, slurp wine and enjoy licking our fingers. Light dims outside, inside candles are lit and I begin playing the piano and to sing a little. But they all know that, while this is perfection, what is happening now, they must go back, though altered and differently fed.

Girls, inmates, all of you, us. We have to fly! calls Violet, echoed by Blanche and by me (a couple of cadences on Charcot's piano first) and by Bertha. It is a rabble out there. Dim and misty the night, but now a man in a fine suit walks directly towards Blanche, seems to know her; eyes shine in acceptance and familiarity. It is Augustine, dressed as she was when she escaped from the Salpêtrière and all those years of being thought the great neurologist's mistress. She had been the queen before Blanche, but no man's whore, she.

Come with me, Blanche. I have a place to go.

Augustine, how did you know where I would be?

Oh, a little bird told me, as I suppose it told you. A letter dropped through the air and landed at my door. I do not live in the finest place, but I have shelter and make enough money with my music.

Come with me, as if you were my wife, even.

Never a wife!

A friend, then. Someone who understands.

A decision has to be made. Go, Blanche, commands Violet: At least for a while. Augustine escaped and was not found. Tonight, may the same be true of you.

Feasts, yes. But love, so much love, too. A tousled bed and a full night.

And with this, our rabble dissolves into the night as Augustine and Blanche, a decent enough couple, though not decorous enough for these parts, walk back towards the Luxembourg Gardens where, on their onward journey to a tawdry apartment, they fade from view. Blanche opens up like a flower; Augustine was luminous: this is how liberty is, but only for the just.

We left his beautiful house in a great mess, says Violet. Rose sweetmeats trampled into the rugs and crayfish tails on the piano. Still, the fine manners I learned at Mother's knees and through a well-trained governess didn't keep me out of a lunatic asylum did it all, dear girls? And just now, oh, it was good to be a *sauvage*. And there's no need to translate that, Lucia.

I call back, in the words of the Brillat-Savarin book, *Oh Monsieur! Such dishes we eat only at your house*! At length, Blanche will return to us and that shall be another story to tell. I hope I will meet Augustine again and that we can talk about her time at the place some called the Versailles of Pain.

Something for Violet. Well, she's been listening to and participating in others' reveries, so what for her? Isn't this her book?

Ah. There would have been much else to change, but all I am wanting now is a quiet end and clear sight. I have my eyes on the hereafter and the moss stones and the lakes and the bay. On quiet cells where I can be pierced by prayer; reading Hopkins! Twilight. Mary. Speak to the Lord Jesus for me. I am very forward and I'm impatient with The Blessed Virgin at this point. My liturgy, now, is not even of its time and definitely not ladylike.

Did Hannah really call me a *crone*? By God, Bertha, may she rest in peace and you with her, holding her hand, in your imagination, transfigured by love. But can I remind you that I *kept my title* so I hope she called me *Lady*, too?

Now, as I told you before, I have been reading Florence Nightingale's *Cassandra*. Did you know that Virginia Woolf said it was like screaming, that book of hers? I concur. I heard her at night and what she screamed was my scream too. Up they came, poor old blood-eyed Griffith on nights. I said, Up he comes from Cardiganshire! and he said Carmarthenshire! Same thing, said I and he hesitated. I assume he was trotting through the old adage: this old loon can't tell a hawk from handsaw. *Was I aware of what I said? Could I read a map? Know a purple mountain from a dolphin in Cardigan bay? Could I know that Dr Griffith, hey*? I caught, briefly, a smile and then he sighed: Oh Miss Gibson, you are giving some trouble!

*Lady Gibson*!

I screamed. Of course I screamed. Hollered, *You think it's madness, that pitch? Well go fack yourself doctors, it's jolly well not: it's the right and rational response! And I will not behave like a Lady!*

And also: Do not medicate me. This makes sense! What I am saying?

From his smile of cognisance, Dr Griffith now attended to what was professional and fitting. Something to settle her, nurse please. She is upsetting the other patients, with the volume and then the cursing.

Ha. I just screamed and facked in my sleep, then.

I am Violet Gibson, the Honourable. Of Merrion Square Dublin and Grosvenor Square London and daughter of the Lord Chancellor of Ireland, Member of Parliament and created First Baron Ashbourne. SO THERE.

You can see why I was considered troublesome in asylums.

It won't be long now, I said when I woke, you near me, my Lucy Light—so I want to think only of what comes next, for I am tired. Give me the funeral I want, lay me down and you, girl, I am dead, thou livest, will you report me and my cause aright? Too wordy! Tell the story. Remember me.

I am not innocent, entirely, but I have been so alone. And now, passerines: If—I am quoting Florence Nightingale again: you remember her *Cassandra*?—you knew how gladly I leave this life, how much more courage I feel to take the chance of another, than of anything I see before me in this, you would put on your wedding clothes instead of mourning for me!

Dr Griffith was back in the room, assessing me, to see if I was properly calm; also, I suppose, to check that they had not accidentally becalmed me altogether, sedating an old bird like that and one who, not long ago, they had thought was finally shuffling off. They don't want to kill me accidentally. One should never do that.

For years, the staff here doubted what I said: I am not mad. I am not sorry, exactly, but I am not mad. I won't do it again. I am harmless. Although I couldn't say that if you gave me my Lebel revolver back, I'd not shoot at another tyrant. But I am not mad. Let me be. I will be still, until I die, send me to the nuns, I had told them, and I will contemplate and let my thoughts be relieved by prayer, which pierces so.

*Hamlet's death, that previous bit,* Lucia would have said. Yes. I am pretty confident that Lucia had made it into the room too, clever girl. And that you all, for as long as you could be, were my witnesses.

Prospero's farewell to his magic, said Dr Griffith. The bit about being relieved by prayer.

Florence Nightingale's *Cassandra*, said Nurse Archer. I read that. Thought it was like screaming, rather than writing.

I found out her name, the nurse's, is Nancy. She is from County Roscommon and nurses here with two of her sisters. I wanted to say that I remember a picnic once at Lough Ree and walking in the grounds of Boyle Abbey on a fine June afternoon. But it felt too late. It was as if I had looked at her for the first time. And she'd never told me about her reading. I do hate to say it, for I'm not a modest woman and make few mistakes, yet I underestimated her.

But: Do not interrupt me, said I!

And so continued: The world will be put back some little time by my death.

Isn't that Florence Nightingale again? says Nancy the nurse.

*I can't go on. I will go on.* Cod Beckett! And I say, yes, Lucia, your Sam, but I am short of breath so my final word to *shh* you is that this is the voice of Florence Nightingale's dying woman and she said: The world will be put back some little time by my death... you see I estimate my powers at least as highly as you can; but it is not the death which has taken place some years ago in me, not by the death which is about to take place now. And so is the world put back by the death of everyone who has to sacrifice the development of his or her peculiar gifts to conventionality. My people—this is the dying woman again and this is me, too; Florence turns a long sentence!—were like children playing on the shore of the eighteenth century. I was their hobby-horse, their plaything; and they drove me to and fro, dear souls! Never weary of the play themselves, till I, who had grown to woman's estate and to the ideas of the nineteenth century, lay down exhausted, my mind closed to hope, my heart to strength.

Free-free-oh! divine freedom, art thou come at last? Welcome beautiful death!

Let neither name nor date be placed on her grave, still less the expression of regret or of admiration; but simply the words, I believe in God.

*Have you done, Violet? I mean, you went ON AND ON*, would trill that Naughty Niluna, that Lucia, and then I'd have retorted, Lucia, if I had been the barnacle, I'd not have abandoned you, but would have taken you in hand, girl—but listen: I do believe, *I do*. In God. Girl, in you. In the fire in your brain whether your wordy daddy gave it to you or not. Use it. Finish the book. *You must.* On my grave, though, Lucia, one day, get the words right, then strew meadow flowers and place a little bird. Do this for me?

Lucia would have reflected. Nodded assent. Complicity. Cries and quotes from my passerines!

*So much talent!*

*So many gifts!*

*Such good which you might have done!*

They were thinking about me (as I said, I am not modest) but also about themselves. Attend them! It would be a good end.

And Violet paused. Pale; trembling a little. I suppose she'd given me an idea of what to do, hadn't she, when the last days or hours came? When Violet's breath was jagged and the signs were there, but she was smiling at me, urging me both for herself and for my own future. So God love this woman, she barks out, now, with that day not too far away, herself tremulous and forever a paradox, the following:

Now, Lucia. Quickly. If you were to choose. To choose different things, what might they be? Be quick. I think I am going. At that point, you'll all need to be looking at me, not at you while you sit there all flaky and Wakey! Ha!

So.

So be it.

Something for Lucia? For me? Slowly I begin to describe what I might choose. Choice, as you might have gathered, has not been a key feature of my life until now. I've been spectated upon, curated, chosen for. Now that choice might be alive, it is both luxurious and frightening. But I've had a little time and the encouragement of my friends, so I say that I'd like, perhaps, an engagement of my choosing, not one chosen by Daddy and tidied up by the barnacle, then fallen flat; details unknown: shame like a scimitar, right through. Hourly.

And you know that you don't need the child and the man, oh no. But. A baby. I always loved children, more so after hanging around for years with all these old women! No offence, Lady Gibson, but still, you can't turn a cartwheel! Oh. Better times. To finish the novel, as you would have me do, Violet, a poetry anthology of my own with my own name on, my own face on it, or a dance school. To have my daddy for longer? Had he not been carried off by the sepsis when he was, then I might not have been left behind at the hospital in Ivry, where Giorgio saw me taken, straitjacketed. Though I cannot be sure, I think that once he, Daddy, was gone, trying to rescue me from inside Occupied France was not, for the family, a priority and to have me gone, there was a push because it meant freedom. For them, not me. For the barnacle, for my brother, then my nephew and on and on—and thereon into the future for any Joyce; that's how it seems to me, though I'm not saying I was a pretty prospect and I know I pained them.

I was trouble. But I was *theirs*. So I suppose I also want... I want... Yes, an apology from my family. I think it's all we ever want. I want them to say, 'I was cruel. I was a bad parent. I put The work/The Wake/The home/The drink before you. And then I died before I had a chance to set it right. I stood while you were vanished into a straitjacket.' Especially YOU, Mother. *I didn't visit you: France; England; those years away in Wales, Llanfairfechan, with the soft hand of the Irish nurses from Roscommon ministering to you, daughter. I said you were a burden; a strain. Later I burned your past or locked it up and if I didn't light the match, I watched its glow or smelled its sulphur and I mouthed yes and did nothing.*

That. That is what I want, have always wanted to hear.

But no, I am not saying I was easy company, oh no. I'm not a simpleton. I read about myself; that I was a schizophrenic. At St Andrew's there was some doubt, you know, about my pathology. Actually, I saw numerous specialists: there was doubt aplenty. But it's easier just to make someone a case, with a name, a number and a disease. Don't you think?

And I want to know. So much I want to know.

It's a multitude of mysteries.

I want to see my records. What all those men wrote about me.

There are people I want to know about. The doctor who kept us safe from the eugenicists, we feebles, at the hospital in Ivry during the war. Dr Delmas. That was his name: I have been thinking about him and about it all. How did he do it? If the brutes had got to me, my teeth might have been pulled, blood counted, memory tested and mocked to death. Injected with pentobarbital again and again, like Mussolini's son, until he was no longer for this world. Until I was reduced to rubble and someone's notes.

I want to know. To know exactly. Why did Mother refuse to come and see me. Ever?

My fiancé, as Violet's? What happened to them? Where did they go?

And you do know, reader, that I am not—*I am not*—letting myself off the hook. I will have been difficult. Am I saying I was not ever ill? No. But I've made it plain, as have my friends about their lives, that it would be too simple to say that it was *all me* or *all her*. I have made it plain that the definitions of madness are shifting and, sometimes, prompted by convenience. Hell, by the patriarchy. But most of all, I am just saying that I want the hand of a parent and for a crinkled-up eye to assure me, *You are my child and I am sorry.*

*I am sorry.*

So a world dissolves and is still. Passerines, full throated, are on the wing, happy and never too close to the sun. Let me conclude. It is only right. I'm the one writing all this down and it's clear I'll be the one to set it out in the world, though broken and quaking it might be.

Violet is very quiet now. At some point, we crept back into St Andrew's and to our rooms. I cannot quite explain how it all came to pass. Violet was very tired, ashen in her black crêpe dress, resting on her bed. And Dr Griffith said: Now Lucia, I think you'd better go and feed the birds on your own. Nurse Archer will keep an eye from the window.

Yes, shortly before dusk I went out. Rushed beauty surrounded me and a swallow swooped to the eaves of the hospital and I thought of Fra Angelico's painting and Lady Gibson's winged helpers. Sometimes that pretty bird was in *The Annunciation*; sometimes, I felt, he slipped away to see Violet. Isn't *that* an entrancing conceit?

# 15

I am quiet here alone. Sad too. Touch, touch me.

James Joyce, *Ulysses*.

I f I were to blow my own trumpet or write my own bill, what might I halloo? *It is Miss Lucia Joyce! She sings; she flies. Miss Lucia Joyce. Dancer, writer. Fine of lettrine and illumination. Beautiful, isn't she? And richer still, with more confident plumage, when not confined or overly drugged with physic.* Well...

But yes, it is Lucia. Violet, darling, it is Lucia. This is your testament, my friend, Violet. And I am as your daughter. You saved me. You did it. You made me see another way, if I were imaginative and would believe in my own self. Anna O—Bertha as you were and as you are, Blanche—Marie as you were and as you are, if you change your mind. This is how it ends and how I remain. Oh, the adventure we had! Some of it was a swerving black, I know, but Oh! I will never stop dreaming of you, or of us all.

And I was thinking about us and our song and, of course, the journeys we had. Essential in that drear place, the asylum. Now. By that hateful but majestic sideboard by the screened lifts in St Andrew's there was a bookshelf. On it were hobby books. Making; watching; collating. Here, *Birds of Britain and Northern Europe* by James Joyce and Nora Barnacle! I saw an avocet wrest one out, a barnacle, once, Mother, barnacle. From a rock. Slurp it went, up and you were gone. I jest. But I am angry; *I remain angry.* That's sanity! But here's another; part jest, part axiom. Did you know that they once thought geese came from the barnacle? Like Dr Griffith, I have read some abstruse books. Oh yes, Gerard's *Herbal*; Violet has it and showed it to me. But I found out that the Holy Roman Emperor Frederick II had a barnacle examined and found no evidence of a bird-like embryo in it. And now I am crying and realise I am rambling-mad as Violet and I must be seen to hold it together. Because when your imagination or the associations you make between ideas become too lickety-split, well, medical professionals look at you askance.

Like I said, I am angry. And I'm bloody sane as day. Excited, too.

Lucy Light. That's what Violet called me, after *Finnegans Wake*, Daddy. She also thought of me as the song thrush, when she names us, her passerines. Visible in flight. Its call: *sipp*! Alarm: rapid, repeated and scolding *tchuk-tchuk-tchuk*. And its song! Loud and sustained, very characteristic sets of phrases and repeated two to four times. Like the movements of a dancer.

Violet. The sparrow. Mostly sedentary (well of course; hard to bounce like a high-hatted lover when medically becalmed and getting on: dicky heart, scant of breath: behind bars); sociable; noisy; chirruping. I think that was, is you. Rather than the sharp repeated *teck* of the tree sparrow. But you loved them both!

Blanche. The robin. Flanks warm buff. Its call a scolding *tic-tic* and a high-pitched *tswee*. Its song is melodious, a melancholy marble. I wrote that as marble, thinking of that fine white breast in Brouillet's painting. I mean *warble*. Freudian slip. Bloody men.

Bertha. Anna O. The nightingale. Skulking, so hard to see. And we didn't see you, did we? Until twenty years after your death. You kept yourself hidden all those years, who and what you were. Splendid song, rich melodious phrases, trills, whistles, a recurring group of *chooc chooc chooc* and your flute-like, higher pitched, *pioo pioo pioo*. *Naughtingel*, as my father would have you. You know, in the incandescent poetry of *The Wake*.

171

Reader. Later, we buried her, Violet Albina Gibson, the Honourable, poor wonderful victorious thing.

I said to her grave: Violet, it is Lucia. Lucia Anna. Syracusa; all sorts. Daddy. I saw him again. Beckett, too. Came from France. But how did I see Daddy if he were dead? Ah well, read on. You will see how strong I am now—so if something is gone, or taken, I set it straight in my mind and see it clearly. *It's real* and don't go saying that's madness or I'll shoot. Or have at you with the mop like you did that old fustian, Miss Drool.

Violet. In the end, I got out. And I mean properly.

My novel and the poems, all with my lettrines. I made them and I finished them so they were whole. Again, sweet you, read on. I taught dance again, as I had been instructed by Margaret Morris in France. I taught children, new mothers. I was *not* too old and my body came to feel lithe; I sloughed off the flaccid weight of older years, as it would settle, as it does for all the women, in Northampton, the forever place, where I could not run or argue because I had to be obedient and sprinting looked like escape; a mad dance like an episode. And my medications: while they calmed me, their doses were generous, I think and I felt, then, my body waste and my thought ossify because I was on slow speed. I was becoming Miss Drool and it terrified me.

But Violet. You had given me hope. I talked to them, our carers, officials, made them listen. Them. Griffith. Area medical board: the men in charge. I was reasonable. Could we reduce my drugs and see how I did? Could we try? Could we have a plan? I remembered what Bertha had said about how she was effective in her work although she was never wholly well, not always, but well enough and full of purpose. As I said, I was reasonable and, in the end, slowly, slowly, they listened to a request for parole.

When that funny old loon (the Honourable) whispered through the walls and made me rage; when she took me outside the first enclosures to her little gravel corner and I saw the passerines and together we fed them. I saw a nuthatch and I gulped cold winter air and swam in it. Had a sense of life anew, a salty day, a Galway Bay. I was lucid, and I was his, my daddy's, Lucia. I was not a genius like him but by God, I was clever and that clever had been wasted. Violet, with her jokes, books, and her little bird on a Fra Angelico pillar, had seen me who I was; seen me as the crossword to my father, but began to solve me.

Oh yes. My gutturals like furrows, as she had them, well now they hid thought and time; when I came to St Andrew's, the boredom and the casting off—one so still as to scream like Cassandra, the other so painful, its hideous rejection, mother, brother, man, woman—as to be unspeakable, ah, couldn't mouth it. What I wanted and how I might get it. There is a sort of sadness which stops your mouth. But she, Violet, with her words to the birds released something in me. First I screamed like Cassandra as Virginia Woolf had it, then I knew song and the creatures of the air. And in their song, which spoke first only to her, to Violet, flowed hope and the light foot of a dance. I calmed; I stopped mangling the language. I also turned away from my defence of mutism and took brave steps forward. They, doctors, nurses, all, began to listen to me. And still I had friends. What harm could I do?

There was news. Marvellous news. Oh, Violet, something happened. Dropped through the air, came a letter from New York: the offer of work and to be an ambassador for me. It was a letter of love and a record of faith in me by someone who, like Violet, thought I was whole. From Frances Steloff, the inimitable New York bookshop owner who knew Daddy. She got to hear of me. Some part from you, Violet? I don't know. Slowly, gradually, they decided I was better. I mean, better enough. Medicated and monitored just so, but better enough, thus I went steady on the psychogenics. Friends of our family came forward: I thought they had all gone, but now I think it was the hope that brought them forward and made me see them. Does that make sense at all?

I lived some years without you, Violet, but you stayed in me. That day, brilliant rime on the gates, lemon sun against the mist,

Anna Livia Plurabelle, well well well! *She went out*. Before I did, though, I changed a few things and we'll come to that.

In New York, I went to work at Gotham Book Mart, as had been suggested by our friend, Frances Steloff. 51 West 47th, 41 West 47th, 16 East 46th! Just saying this, writing it. Numbers, movement, streets to shift down, that freedom is so very delicious. Move a girl, a book, a shop, a mind. It was their bookstore, the Steloffs, but even when Frances sold it, she kept working there, that was how much it meant and how much she loved it. Move a girl, a book, a shop, a mind. The people I saw! And I could talk to them! Yes, sometimes it was too much, but the world had begun to exude possibility and I could rally, with rest and friendship. But most of all *this*. The bookshop, as you might know, was where they curated The James Joyce Society ten years before I got out. Then Frances was its treasurer and Mr T.S. Eliot its first member. You know, that fellow you pointed out when we were in Switzerland? There on the waters, with Viv, for his nerves? Apologies. Digression? But we are all ill sometimes; maybe all mad: no-one is immune. Why would you think otherwise? It's just redaction and gall, not to admit it, I think.

I couldn't speak of him—to others I mean—of Daddy yet, so I listened, but give it time. Then I was bolder, came down my extraordinary father's cold red road and I read to them, at the bookshop, from his *Pomes Penyeach*. I rehearsed so hard A Flower Given to My Daughter—*Too much, too much, but you can do it Lucia!* consoled Violet, in my head, in my heart, willing me on—so I managed. I said *Love, hear thou* from his work and I was mouthing only of Daddy when I said... when I said (of course I am crying, I am crying)... *I was a wonder wild.*

And the audience said *Was that you, in the poem?* and I said, was proud, *Why yes I believe it was.*

To still me, after I had listened and read to these reverent guests who so valued my father, I wrote poems of my own: *Pomes Dolereach.* Do you like it, the title? I know it to be a little silly, but you, Violet, loved jokes and never gave them up, even on your deathbed. One day my poems might be read by anyone, but as they are now, they are only for him and for my latter-day friend. I enjoy playing now, again, with lettrines and illuminations, but also I know the harm a book can do, after all. So I'm cautious. Mostly.

Oh and this is how I saw Daddy again. I read him aloud, let him inspire me and so called him into being. Don't say that's madness.

No.

It's imagination and love.

Here's a thought for you all, too. Jung was an interesting fellow. In a way, I wish we'd kept up. I knew he was on a quest for self-exploration; he was uneasy and searching. And he had much to say about madness. So here: Madness, said he, is a special form of the spirit and clings to all teachings and philosophies, but even more to daily life, since life itself is full of craziness and at bottom utterly illogical. Man strives toward reason only so that he can make rules for himself. Life itself has no rules. That is its mystery and its unknown law. What you call knowledge is an attempt to impose something comprehensible on life. You see, I learned to abide by the rules of the mental hospital in order to be quiet and to be able to leave. But beyond that, *who are you kidding*? None of us knows what we are up to! I see as clearly as I am able and I enjoy the mystery of it all, just as Violet encouraged me to do.

Oh yes and Sam Beckett. Well I really saw him. Actually, we could lose the adverb because really is subjective, isn't it? You know, it's *all* mystery and unknown law! But yes, Sam came to me in Paris, where I went next. No, not another affair; he was betrothed then to Susanne. But he listened to my work and encouraged me and was cordial. I was proud.

And my novel. *My Work in Progress*. I had almost completed it before but it had been wrested from my head and hand and I do not know by whom. Psychotropics? Phenothiazines?

Hypnotics? Sedatives? Mother or Giorgio? That cross boy my nephew. Does it matter? I will finish that one day; it's well on the way in its draft form. I started all over again. About flight; freedom. Of course.

I am thinking aplenty, but now thinking is not always frightening. Life is not easy, but I am free: not Poor Isa, not poor Dilly, sister of my father's Stephen Dedalus. I can travel, not be a sacrifice to someone or some thing. I am educated, a polyglot and I have the words and the dance. But yet, oh yet. But still voyaging to work out who or what I am, in a mad swerve that belongs to me and only to me. You remember what you said now Violet, I hope?

*That those who are confined have the best imaginations.*

His work sold. Daddy's. Of course. As we knew, he was a genius. But I was not, *was* I? Though as Violet knew, my imagination was rich. Yours is too. *Test it.*

Could we be geniuses together? *Try?* You'd better be a testy virago, though I am open to offers.

As I was saying, his work sold. *It sold.* Some days so well that I raged because barnacle and Daddy birthed me in penury, immured me, and I think, I can't go on, I will go on. And so on and on. They let me have a little money from the estate; the stuff that, I suppose, would have been spent by mother and Giorgio on keeping me inside. And I earn some, too. I can travel, times away from my work in Paris, helping the children and the new mothers to heal and dance and feel joy and strength, as Margaret Morris would, so she had trained me, have me do. I wanted, I needed to go back to Paris, so I spent days, too, at Shakespeare and Company Bookshop. Gradually, I would write more, in my *Work In Progress*, my novel, or another book, if need be, my own *Wake*, of the Paris of my girlhood. But as I was saying, Shakespeare and Co. It used to be called *Le Mistral* and that's a word I have always loved. *Mistral.* So. I have had time to spend with Sylvia Beach, founder of the original bookshop of this name, at 12, Rue de l'Odéon and the one person brave enough to take on my father's *Ulysses*. Wait: there is a plaque for her. Good. Dance. Lucia. Dance for your daddy.

EN 1922 DANS CETTE MAISON
M'ELLE SYLVIA BEACH PUBLIA
'ULYSSES'
DE JAMES JOYCE.

J.J.S.S.F.

Do you know that in 1941—and my father had died eleven months before, yes, and I only heard it on my radio in hospital (can you imagine? Giorgio, barnacle did not tell me)—a Nazi officer went into her shop and insisted that she sell him the last copy of *Finnegans Wake*? She would not sell it.

*It is not for sale.*

*Yes it is for sale it is in your shop.*

*No, still it is not for sale.*

*I am getting angry SELL IT TO ME THIS INSTANT.*

*No it is not for sale.*

And he, brute, told her that he would confiscate everything in her shop and close it down. She was majestic. I heard that she took everything upstairs to an apartment. Do you know that Sylvia Beach spent six months in an internment camp at Vittel? She hid the book. Left it on the roof, in a nest box, brown waxed paper, a sturdy bag on top and safe, so a little bird told me, and I have it now. My dear copy of *Finnegans Wake*. It says *Lucy Light* at its beginning. Came Sylvia home, to this lovely place. She told me she hadn't written the inscription so... who did? Well now I think that, somehow, it was you, Violet. But how on earth? That secret went with you. Like I said before, there's a multitude of mysteries.

Sometimes I stay at Shakespeare and Company, a tumbleweed: that's what they are called. Tumbleweeds. Anyone can tumble in for a while and home up. You browse, read, work among the books and rest there, like one of us and one of them, a sleeping giant, yourself. I do it too. Why don't you come on, too? I sleep there, work in the bookshop for a few hours and if you look at

177

all the one-page autobiographies there—thousands; it is part of being a tumbleweed—you will see mine. It says *Lucia Anna Joyce. Roamer. Daughter of James Joyce. Rager. Artist of sorts, dancer and teacher. Friend. Mistral!*

I was happy with that description and to include the gorgeous blustery word that Blanche had so loved. *Mistral.* Make it apply to me, with all my spirits and the energy that had been bundled under. And Violet, I will make a page for you, too; invite others to comment. I shall keep an eye on that!

And I remember. I shivered when we ran through the streets of Paris, to the feast at the house of Monsieur Charcot and I didn't know why, then. It was because, one day, the bookshop, a home of sorts, would be there, nearby.

These days, I am relaxed about what I believe in, because of everything I learned and which happened, so I'll give prescience a go. Why not?

Before I left the hospital in Northampton, I changed my will because I was free and I had to be sure of what came next. You don't need to be completely better to go out into the world, so I was wary. Dr Griffith helped me. You, Violet had a hunch, didn't you? *Give your wills, your thoughts, to your women.* But for now, I am out and here. I won't be silenced. Now you can know me and always, if that is what you would like. Harriet Weaver, lately Daddy's patron, and her fine, fine goddaughter Jane Lidderdale, made me free. Like I said, friends of our family whom I thought were gone. And I was wrong. And oh, my Violet: while it was too late to save everything, more of my letters are there, so others can see me, or at least more of me, in time to come. We got there before they were *immolated.*

And there's Blanche; Bertha inhabiting the draft of my novel. Violet, you made me your scribe. God love you.

And if you still want to know what my book is about? The novel I mentioned? You are reading it. Well I am sure you grasped that. You're clever. And I am a clever girl. And I don't want Violet to be forgotten. In my head it is called *Work in*

*Progress*, because I am, because he was, dying too soon, because of *The Wake*. But out loud I call it *Saving Lucia* because of Violet, who started the whole shooting match off, extending her hands like Giotto's St Francis with the birds, then making us fly. The book's still drafting; a juddery old thing, but I'm proud of it. Do feel free to write in the margins though. Cross things out if you're just too disbelieving!

Such episodes in our story! Can you believe we did it, that *we* shot Mussolini? Had it been sooner, then there was more that we could all have done. Saved Matteotti, leader of the Socialist party, whom he had butchered, two years before our Lebels were raised. No-one should fail to come to their family. Be found in a ditch. The many unspoken, but known and loved. It is too big to grasp, what things in time to come may not be. Abyssinia I know of. And his Augustan Empire: the glittering things he held proud; times in other countries. Different, yes? Originally, thus: Il Duce's wife arrested and, like us, committed to a mental hospital. The rest of her life was a nightmare of escapes, re-arrests and attempts to trace her son. He, emperor, had made sure she had enough pain to break her. This boy: adopted by the former Fascist police chief of Sopramonte. Ida Dalser died, they said, of a brain haemorrhage in 1937 at a Venetian institution. I think they took her off, but only after she'd died of the crying. Her son went five years later, also in an institution, near Milan. They injected and injected and kept him in a coma. His heart gave way, they said. You heard all this earlier. Now I want to say, *Not in our story, oh no.* How should a soul be capable of such cruelty?

At Coppet I had warned her. She was vile to me, if you remember, but as Violet would have stated, 'It is not fair, what they have done.' I suppose you could have said that, when he took off her husband in 1926, we'd made her safe, but you couldn't be sure. He was already plotting and planning, cronies all about; she already chirping. So I was glad to warn; to note that she'd listened.

But I cry at night. *We couldn't save everyone.*

But we'd done for himself, for bad bird Benito, hadn't we?

Bang. This time, four Lebel revolvers. Square on Campidoglio. Then we were gone, on the wing. Who killed Cock Robin? He who thought he was cock of the wark? *We* did.

So.

Oh enormous things happened because of what we did. It all starts with the freedom, in mind, of the individual and no son should be motherless, just as—and I am sorry, Daddy, for saying this—no mother should be without her son, as Helen Kastor Joyce your daughter in law was when you took the little child from her, my brother, my Giorgio, my one time adventurer, my captain fey on Galway Bay. My. *Stop.* You are already gone. You all did wrong. I do have some tenderness, but on my raging Dilly Days, then I might come out and eat Mother and son and sometimes Daddy with bacon and spice, like the tripe so loved by Rabelais, and I would eat all three, a Pantagruelian dish, until I had bad indigestion. Blanche: she said something like this about her spectators at the Salpêtrière. Such gargantuan intrigues. Get your napkin! What a feast we had, at the house of Charcot. But I am sorry. It is only in words that I make my violence and calm my appetites now; it was really all I wanted.

That—and love. And I came to love you Violet. You were not, could not be, my friend so long and I could not change your time to go because you were tired and frail and off, helter skelter, so you said, to see your Maker and roast the bad priests and a few others. You told all this, in the last days. They never understood how funny you were, God love you.

Oh! you said: Do it right, miss. You might be St Lucy but you're also Anna the putative Mother of The Virgin Mary, so what would be your excuse now? Oh dear girl, silly girl.

I answered you back, though you were dying. Oh! I mocked a little, because I said *Shh now, old girl!* but I loved you. Then, I told you there was a painting I had been thinking about. I said: And do you know that, in a painting by Jacobello del Fiore that

I once saw in Fermo, Italy, St Lucy is kneeling before the shrine of St Agatha. I'm going in hard now Violet, but that's alright. St Agatha had her breasts removed; you, too, suffered such levelling, such scars. And you told me that you shot yourself there, too. The things you have suffered, in illness, in violence and in such deep sadness. I thought about that painting, then about you and, in my dreams some nights ago, St Peter the Apostle came to you in prison and healed you. Now... well my friend, it is as if much of life, the paintings I saw, words I swallowed, were like a prefiguration of times to come; time with you. Is it like you and me, in a way, that painting? And were you, in a prison, healed?

I was crying, obviously. You were leaving, but you, old bird, looked at me and I heard a throaty little giggle and you trilled: Well now Lucia, *you* decide. Go inland dear girl. What does your imagination tell you? Then you pulled me close and said: Promise you will remember?

It was only *I* that heard this one. I, said the song thrush.

Outside flew the lark, the goldfinch, nuthatch and the modest little sparrow.

I.

Elsewhere, saved, robin, nightingale.

And then Violet was at peace. You *were*, my Lady.

You got Mass. I made sure of that. I am Lucy Light and know a thing or two about persuasion.

The priests were there, just as you'd wanted. The censer clicked and I thought I heard you cackle. The lover and the damask rose and the scent of jasmine; I sensed you swooning with these memories. I'd listened so carefully to you and you were not what they thought you were. I imagined more things for you.

I thought, I'd done it again just before we lost you.

Tried to make moments for you. You had said that you'd like a few little things before you left us, so it went: your fiancé back, one time. Brothers: Victor, Willie, Harry, the champion tobogganer; a new painting by De Maistre took place at brother Willie's place in France and this time you were looking up and sister Constance, who was dutiful, holding your hand. In all the photographs taken at St Andrew's, as the birds came to you, not once did you or could you face the camera. This was different, as you posed for De Maistre's initial sketch: you faced the artist head on and without shame. I wondered if Blanche had whispered to you about that! *Show yourself for who you are*, she might have said. *Or show yourself for how you wish or need to be seen*! Yes, I am glad that, as you died, I could tell all these stories to you. Create these moments, when you were supine and comfortable.

You had said to me: We fly, Passerines. Lucia, dear girl, I imagine we will be buried in different places, but please make them give us our Mass, and listen to what we both want. Have yourself buried by your daddy, in Zurich, if you want. Put our graves with the proper inscriptions: take yours from your daddy, if you will, but make mine from the nightingale, the lark or the goldfinch. I do not mind. Don't let mine be plain, sweet mad girl! But not overwrought, either. After the comma there must be text; I think that they, whoever attends to my grave, may leave it unfinished, but after mad I shall need something new.

And the birds came, as we sang into the dust. Passerines. I was better, gradually, then. I thought that Dr Griffith might listen to me. As you saw, he did. Got others to, like I said. Official folk, you know. Poor old Dr Griffith must have been in such an imbroglio that night at St Andrew's when we caused chaos just before our flight. That night, when down the corridors of the asylum echoed a turbulent commotion and alarms flew. This was the bit the staff heard, but they'd missed the whispers, glissando of the winged helpers no louder than a heartbeat through a greatcoat; rustles of paper and scratches of soft pencil. A tremendous thing. Nothing could have stopped it then. Poor man. We must have given him a fright!

And Dr Griffith kindly spoke to those who remained, to your executor, Violet, about the headstone. More words were allowed, so on the stone it went, it fluted, *I fly to thee.*

I wanted to add all kinds of this and that, but I told myself no. But still, it seemed a bit melancholy, so on I went, and now it said,

THE HONOURABLE VIOLET ALBINA GIBSON,

1876-1956.

Even the sparrow finds a home and the swallow a nest.

I fly to thee.

In my head, it also said *I shot Mussolini* which was better than the drear record of your failed attempt in *Burke's Peerage*— Went to Rome in 1926 and tried to assassinate Mussolini by shooting—but so.

Violet, I will *not* have you forgotten.

That day you died, Dr Griffith confided in me; he said: I was a scripture champion you know. In Carmarthenshire, turn of the century. He was tired and wizened, but I thought that he had learned from you, Violet. And when you were slipping away and I was allowed to see you, hold your hand, he stood near me. I had said *I promise to remember, Honourable lady.* And I saw Griffith and his eyes were moist. He stood on his own, turning round to look at the wide sweep of lawns and that little spot where the birds flew to you, Violet. Could he see all assembled company in the room? He'd missed some prime case studies there!

Love always, Blanche; Bertha. I'll not forget.

These fellows. All those you have heard described. They must wonder what their life's work has come to be, wrestling us in and out of our rooms, penning us up in Caliban's cave while they wait to prescribe from their cabinet and chart. But I know that's not entirely fair. Dr Delmas, from the asylum in Ivry-sur-Seine, where I was at the beginning of the war, in Vichy France. I would like to see him again, one day, if it were possible (and as we know, possible can be stretched). We owe him our safety, still, because the Nazis were marauding, weeding out the feebles like me, like I came to know I was; the lunatics. When I am as strong as I can be, I want to find out. Another book to write, maybe? But on one thing, Dr Delmas was wrong: suicide is not caused only by insanity. Despair, rage, cage: this is also what I saw. When we are made prisoners, we go mad, if we were not before and, as I think we have all said, prisons are plural and various.

There is something else, though, and it bothers me night and day. If we killed Mussolini, we neither saved Hannah Karminski, Bertha's beautiful work, nor killed Hitler. There was so much more to do, once we took the bad bird, once we shot the monster, that it breaks my heart. Bear witness to this: are you a madwoman or do you know one? Commune with others and shoot. I still have my Lebel. I've bought more, in fact.

*Take them.*

*If you find tyrants. If it's the only way.*

When I got out—of St Andrew's Northampton, I mean—and I don't mean I escaped, like Augustine from the Salpêtrière: no, I was discharged, as I told you—I went first to your grave, Lady Gibson, and I took you something: a little swallow, then I added a sparrow, clever and tight-bound little ornaments. The birds with which you and only you communed gave us back our lives, mad girls, at different hours. Why don't you, reader, go and see it? As you bear witness in reading, you are part of this story too, aren't you now? I haven't made up such detail. The grave was half-planned to be so plain; I could not bear it and was glad to help here. I suspect mine will be pretty, or at least shiny and expensive, though God knows where it'll go. Near my friend? I've a flexible idea of home. Violet, you always said we would be buried near each other. Could that be true?

Could it? You had said: Ah Syracusa! You'll get your pretty granite, alright. But don't go expecting Zurich! I wanted to hit out at you. No tact and remarkably little grace for an Honourable, sometimes.

And yet. Oh God, what grace. What grace and understanding. Violet Albina Gibson. The Honourable. Yes, you saved me.

******

Did all this really happen? Of course. But what do you know, who has not been mad? *You must believe it,* for I am a weird, haughty, naughty, beautiful Niluna of *Finnegans Wake*. I am my father's daughter. Violet Gibson was not just part of history. She *was* history and she changed it with the birds of the skies and a polish of the cross she held up as she died; the detail she noticed and the imagination she sustained. I know this is a lot to take in, but a metamorphosis was hers and she let us help her. And we love her.

*Remember.*

Write, talk, fly, sing.

Don't doubt her. Were *you* on the radio, immortalised in song? No? *Well then.*

Flanagan: Listen to this. Cricket. Ashes for England after fourteen years.

Allen: Irish woman, Violet Gibson, shoots Mussolini in the nose.

*Remember.* You'll do that for me.

Won't you?

Thank you.

God love you reader, and, like I said, feel free to annotate the margins of this Work in Progress. This strange story of women who lived and laughed and loved and left.

# Acknowledgements

I am grateful to the archivist at St Andrew's Hospital, Northampton, who was quick to help me with information because, at the time of writing, the archives were closed as part of their move to storage elsewhere. For this book, my love and thanks go to my publisher, Bluemoose, and to Kevin and Hetha and my lovely editor Lin Webb. Thank you for all you do.

To my friends. All your kind attentions are too numerous to mention: you know who you are! I'd like to say a particular thank you to Alexi, Sarah and Susie. The encouragement of writers and those in the publishing industry has, again, proved invaluable, so special thanks to Peter Fullagar, who read the manuscript and talked it through with me, and especially to Heidi James for reading and cheerleading; to J. Hall, Ariel Kahn, Kate Armstrong, Alex Campbell and Avril Joy. For Kate Johnson, Julia Silk and also all at Influx Press, especially Gary Budden. For Thom and Sam at Dodo Ink. Stu Hennigan, Steve Clough and Lucie McKnight Hardy. Heartfelt thanks to Jordan Taylor-Jones. And for Sophie and Dave on the occasion of their marriage, Wiltshire, September 2018, with much love.

Thank you to our NHS. It is hard to get and maintain help, but I have always battled mental health problems and it is there, an enduring comfort to me. MHRS: God love you.

And an enormous thank you to my three boys, Elijah, Isaac and Caleb and to my husband, Ned, who insisted I write this book and read and corrected anachronisms with a clear eye; the title was also his. All errors rest with me. This book is, above all, for you, my darling, because most things are.

# Afterword and a very special thank you

At the beginning of this book there is a dedication to nursing sisters of Roscommon. There is a reason for this: during the writing of this book, something extraordinary happened. I had been trying to find out where Lucia Joyce had gone in her time away from St Andrew's and discovered that, during the Blitz, some patients were evacuated to Bryn y Neuadd at Llanfairfechan in North Wales, which at the time was a sort of sister hospital. And through information on Bryn y Neuadd, I found Kevin O'Hara, the American writer and former psychiatric nurse, who told me that his mother and two aunts had nursed Violet Gibson in St Andrew's. There were family stories handed down. His Aunt Nancy was still alive and ninety-five. She and her sisters had emigrated to America and from there Nancy, the remaining sister, shared information with me. Violet had been a great favourite of Kevin's mother and aunts. Kevin wrote: "'Lady Gibson rarely spoke to anyone,' Mom told us, "but one morning, out of the blue, she asked if I'd help her sew little pouches into the shoulders of her black dress. She'd go filling these pouches with breadcrumbs and sit perfectly still in the rose garden, where sparrows and redbreasts would alight on her shoulders and begin to feed. She did this for years, mind you, and we'd often tell her that her cheeks had been caressed by the wings of a thousand birds, and our words never failed to make her smile.'" When I had this information, Violet Gibson felt finally... real.

While I was in Northampton I visited Kingsthorpe Cemetery, where Violet is buried a few footsteps away from the grave of Lucia Joyce. I placed on Violet's grave a small bird: a sparrow—a passerine, like the birds coming to her hands. And also a swallow, another passerine, like the one on Fra Angelico's pillar, which was sometimes there and sometimes not. And that was just from me, though if you recall, Violet asks Lucia to put a little bird there for her, so maybe...

You *were* history, Violet. And you definitely changed my life.

# Reading and sources

This is a work of fiction based on real people; what follows is just a small selection of my own reading. *The Woman Who Shot Mussolini* by Frances Stonor Saunders (Faber and Faber, 2011), a biography of Violet Gibson, is a wonderfully sensitive portrait of Violet Gibson side by side with a riveting one on Mussolini and on contemporary history. *Lucia Joyce: To Dance In The Wake*, by Carol Loeb Shloss (Farrar, Straus and Giroux, New York, 2003) attempts, painstakingly, through reconstruction and close reading of *Finnegans Wake*, to allow a reader to see the father's love for his daughter and reveal her. The article 'Nineteenth-Century Hysteria and Hypnosis: A Historical Note on Blanche Wittmann' by Carlos S. Alvarado in *Australian Journal of Clinical and Experimental Hypnosis* (volume 37, no.1, 2009, pages 21-36) led me on to many contemporary or near contemporary accounts of Charcot at the Salpêtrière. There are many accounts one might read of the past treatment of women in psychiatric institutions; based on her study of cases from the Homewood Retreat, Cheryl Krasnick Warsh concluded, in *Moments of Unreason: The Practice of Canadian Psychiatry and The Homewood Retreat, 1883-1923* (McGill-Queens University Press, 1989) that 'the realities of the household in late Victorian and Edwardian middle-class society rendered certain elements—socially redundant women in particular—more susceptible to institutionalization than others'. Whether women were mentally ill or if their families wanted to silence opinion, it was not so difficult to send them to mental institutions, thus rendering them vulnerable and submissive.

In 1887 (when Violet would have been ten), the American journalist Nellie Bly had herself committed to the Women's Lunatic Asylum in New York City, as 'Nelly Brown', in order to investigate conditions there. Her account was published in the 'New York World' newspaper, and in book form as *Ten Days in A Mad-House* (the pamphlet was published by Ian L. Munrow, New York and can be read online at digital.library. upenn.edu/women/bly/madhouse/madhouse.html). The text is full of descriptions such as this, as the author goes about her routine of the day: 'I looked at the poor crazy captives shivering, and added, emphatically, "It's horribly brutal."'

On Mussolini, Richard Bosworth's *Mussolini* (London, 2002) is fascinating reading, but *The Woman Who Shot Mussolini* (above) tells the story of Violet and Mussolini side by side and I would recommend both, one after the other. Also Christopher Duggan's *The Force of Destiny. A History of Italy since 1776* (London, 2007). Blanche is discussed in Asti Hustvedt *Medical Muses: The Culture of Hysteria in Nineteenth-Century Paris* (W.W. Norton and Company, 2011) and Bertha in a full biography, *The Enigma of Anna O. A Biography of Bertha Pappenheim* by Melinda Guttmann (Moyer Bell and Subsidiaries, 2001). I have drawn on *Selected Letters of James Joyce* (ed Richard Ellmann, Viking Press, New York, 1975), the work of James Joyce in the various editions in which I had it, folklore, Dante, the Bible, Jewish history and sacred texts, the works of Samuel Beckett in the editions in which I own them; also stories by Hans Christian Andersen. And the texts of Freud, Breuer and Jung, John Clare, writings on saints and Fra Angelico and, of course, I looked everywhere for birds!